VACATION

AND
OTHER TALES
OF
ENDURING LOVE

Also by Glenn Morrow

Things Beloved: Two Short Novels
"The Observatory"
"The Better Boat"

Selected as a Best Book of 2023

"I was happily blown away by the tight, smart prose, especially in the second of the two novellas, which is about a boy who finds a sailboat half buried in the sand and restores it. I found the story spare and intensely moving. This book is like a secret treasure—a real find."—Christina Lynch, author of *The Italian Party* and *Pony Confidential*

"These stories are imbued with justice and in the end, comfort. I laughed and sighed and recognized myself. Morrow writes with grace and clarity. In his assured, unfolding stories, I was carried in his wisdom. He respects and loves his characters. I can't wait to see whatever else Morrow turns his pen to."—Cynthia Linkas, author of *Vows* and *Tumbled Time*

"What do an obsolete observatory and a rudderless sailboat have in common? Or a handful of middle-aged university alumni with an eager twelve-year-old boy? Both of the objects face demolition; both are beloved. The former undergraduates remain awed by their old discoveries under the observatory dome; young Anthony, his heart racing, is spellbound by the wonders of his boat. Consummate story-teller Glenn Morrow roots his characters in compassion and spikes his words with grace and wit. This is a book for those of us who hunger for stories that celebrate our innate generosity and goodness, while we greedily turn the pages. Two stories, one slim book for everyone's bedside table."—Sally Ryder Brady, author of *A Box of Darkness: The Story of a Marriage*

"If you want tales that intrigue, surprise, amuse, and move you, look no further than *Things Beloved*. Morrow's work brings you close to real people in extraordinary situations facing challenging moral choices. He writes with engaging skill and resonant empathy."—R.C. Binstock, author of *What You Can't Give Me* and *Tree of Heaven*

"The heart and the intellect dance an intimate tango of wit and wisdom in Glenn Morrow's stories that allow us the hope of personal and communal justice and redemption in the ordinary and extraordinary circumstances of life."—Kiki Latimer, author of *Seeing God's Face* and co-author of *Philosophy Begins in Wonder*

VACATION
AND
OTHER TALES
OF
ENDURING LOVE

Glenn Morrow

En Route Books and Media, LLC
Saint Louis, MO

⚓ENROUTE
Make the time

En Route Books and Media, LLC
5705 Rhodes Avenue
St. Louis, MO 63109

Contact us at: contactus@enroutebooksandmedia.com

Cover photo credit: Mike Lane, used with permission
Cover design credit: Team Waxwing
Author photo credit: Deborah Morrow
Waxwings quotation: Our Wedding Invitation

ISBN: 979-8-88870-268-0
Library of Congress Control Number: 2024950615

Dedication

For my wife Deborah, life companion on this journey, best inspiration, and closest reader.

In grateful memory of my parents, Chris and Jeanette, and the gift to us of their enduring love for each other. And in thanks to God for the blessed strong marriages of our children.

Acknowledgments

To be a writer is to build imaginary gardens and populate them with real frogs. I am indebted to my writers' groups, companions in creativity, for any coherence that may have resulted. Specific mention must be made of Sally Brady's Writers' Group, The Stone House Writers' Retreat, and the Willett Free Library Writers' Group, and the following individuals: R.C. Binstock, Chris Cassaday, Bob Dutson, Pam Floyd, Angela Gerst, Susan Hammen-Winn, Alice Holstein, Anna Kovel, James Lansill, Christina Lynch, Jeffrey Lewis, Mary Mitchell, Chris Todd Morrow, James Morrow, Kate Risse, Larry Rothstein, and Mike Scott. Sally Brady, literary midwife, has nurtured my writing for years and I gratefully acknowledge her influence in every clear sentence. The several errors that have undoubtedly persisted are entirely mine. Sebastian Mahfood and Kiki Latimer were instrumental in getting this work into print.

Table of Contents

Waxwings

Waxwings

In courtship, a pair of waxwings perch on a branch side by side, one holding a berry in its beak. The birds then pass the fruit back and forth. After each transfer, the receiving bird hops away, then back to its original position before returning the berry. The pair repeats these actions several times, each mirroring the other. Mutual and reciprocal, it tokens more than simple nurturance. For when berries are scarce, they perform the same dance with the petals of a flower.

Mr. Coe's Garden

"Curtis, bring me a sack of dynamite and fifty feet of fuse."

By then, I had gotten used to Mr. Coe's language. So I got him what he asked for: plant fertilizer and a garden hose. I was fifteen (almost sixteen). I had no idea how old Mr. Coe was, but he was impossibly old. So old as to seem like an entirely different species, like a land tortoise or a great blue heron. Totally too old to be planting an enormous garden. But that was what he was determined to do.

That high school summer I helped Mr. Coe create a backyard-sized jungle of green plants and blooming flowers. But it didn't start that way. When I first showed up to do "yard work" I thought I'd be mowing grass and pulling weeds. But Mr. Coe had other ideas.

He wanted me to destroy his lawn. He had me rip up every inch of the grass behind his house and pile it against the stockade fence. A lawn that had probably grown there for, like, ages. And for sure the only things that disturbed it before were squirrels burying nuts, lawn mowers, and dandelions.

My first week was nothing but scraping up turf. The work was harder than I was used to. Running JV Track was no preparation for this stuff. And the payoff was blisters and bare dirt. I would have quit that Friday, but I couldn't bring myself to do it. Mr. Coe was in just too good a mood.

And, I admit it, I was hypnotized by his bizarre way of talking. Everything had a funny name, which seemingly he invented to keep me, you know, entertained. He referred to the back lawn as "the

7

monoculture," which he pronounced like a Viennese shrink on television: "I'm afrait vot ve've got zeehr ista bad kase oof der *mono-culture*." The good doctor said surgery was the only option.

When it sunk in that the whole lawn was going to go, I thought we were going to make a big vegetable garden, something that made sense. But Mr. Coe said that vegetables belonged in grocery stores. Where you could keep an eye on them.

Before we started using explosives, Mr. Coe and I handled snakes. We used these hissing tape measures to place wooden stakes, laying out paths that would meet in the middle of his big, now pretty-much-empty, back yard. He'd show me where the pegs went, then Mr. Coe would run string between them. He had me pounding them in with an old wooden hammer that nobody makes anymore.

He had everything planned out way in advance on something he called his Treasure Map, a big roll of paper that I could never make any sense of. He kept checking it and then pointing to where he wanted paths and where he wanted plants.

There was going to be a path that went around the edge of what used to be the lawn, then straight paths going from there to the center, dividing up the garden like a pizza. There was nothing in the center, but I figured he was going to do a fountain, or maybe one of those sun things.

I kept tripping over the strings, but Mr. Coe just laughed and replaced the busted twine. I was kinda concerned about old Mr. Coe doing a face plant. But no worries. He seemed to know his way around without hardly looking.

And when the flowers started arriving from the nursery, he introduced them as "ladies," greeting them by their "proper" names, weird mouthfuls of what he told me was Latin. No chance I could remember any of it. But Latin was something spoken like an old-school Roman by thin, angular Mr. Coe.

"Curtis, I'd like you to meet the Zalea sisters: A. Zalea, Bea Zalea, Dee, and Em." Then something with big green leaves he called "Hosta," and he joked about "freeing the hostas" like it was the same word as *hostage*. But I knew it wasn't.

I don't think he ever got that this was just a summer job for me. He talked garden stuff pretty much non-stop, like putting plants in dirt was the most important thing anyone could ever do.

Unlike all the other adults around me, Mr. Coe made no attempt to be my buddy. He never once asked me about school, or sports, or said something lame about social media or gaming. Or asked me what I wanted to be when I grew up. For this I was totally grateful. Instead, our conversations would start with him dropping something from a great height.

"Topiary," he would say. "Take an unsuspecting boxwood. Snip it until it looks like anything but what a boxwood wants to be. Like the head of our former president, or the swirl of a soft serve ice-cream cone—remarkably similar shapes, in my opinion. And how do we feel about topiary?"

"Sounds like we're not big fans."

"Decidedly anti-topiary. A garden shouldn't look like a person's idea of a garden. It should look like a plant's idea of a garden party. Ilex with his sharp opinions, plump Buxus, and Syringa vulgaris, nodding and a tad too fragrant, all come together to mingle and chit-chat in little trios and quartets."

Most of the time I couldn't follow Mr. Coe's thinking. But I figured out that I didn't have to. I could just repeat a couple of his words back to him. "A plant's idea?"

"An exemplary insight, Curtis," he said, as if I had started the whole conversation. "Let's consider that. Not a person's idea of a plant. A plant's idea of itself. Yes. A very worthy thought."

I think that's what happens when you get old.

We worked away for weeks together, and what was a weed patch lawn started turning into something totally other. I was used to the dinky suburban gardens in our neighborhood—bunches of tulips and those yellow flower bushes on the edge of walks. That was hundred percent no preparation for what this old man was doing, filling up every inch of his back yard with strange plants I'd never seen before.

The street front of his house kept its handful of rose bushes dividing the Coe property from the sidewalk. We did exactly zip work on the front. Everything we did happened behind the house, hidden from view by stockade fencing. It was a lot of sweat for something that none of the neighbors were ever going to see. Anyway, at the end of each day he tallied my hours and paid me in cash from a seemingly endless roll of bills.

And every day we ate the same lunch of peanut butter and jelly sandwiches and iced tea at the kitchen table. Then he'd unrolled his Treasure Map and made little check marks with a red crayon.

And then one time he goes: "Mrs. Coe will be delighted with all the good work you've done."

I looked around the old-style kitchen. Since there was nothing that I could see that showed any Mrs. Coe living there, or that anyone like that had ever lived there, I just nodded. We picked up our gardening gloves and went back to work. But as I replaced marking stakes with dug holes (which he called "lacunas"), then filled the shoveled holes with burlap-wrapped root balls, the thought of Mrs. Coe hovered around me like gnats.

Since the garden we were building was sorta formal, I figured she'd be that way too. You know, prim. There would be white gravel walkways for her super-long skirts, sweet-scented flowers high enough for her to, you know, breathe them in, her white glove steadying their stems.

The Mrs. Coe in my imagination could only exist in the garden Mr. Coe was making. There was nobody like that in our neighborhood. Outside the Coe's back yard all the adults that I saw were in ceaseless motion. Up and out early to get to their workouts, then rushing to their offices for Important Meetings. Sneaking off early to dash to an open house tour of real estate they knew they really didn't want, then meeting up for heated games of Pickleball, arguing the whole time about the rules. Mr. Coe wasn't racing around or competing with anybody. He was quietly creating a private garden for the never-present Mrs. Coe.

Just about every day a garden center truck dropped off more burlap bundles with green stalks poking out the top. I hauled them in and lined them up along the fence. They all had to be put in the dirt. It seemed an impossible task. And the plants kept coming. Like maybe he'd forgotten what he ordered and kept getting the same things over and over. Three weeks in the fruit trees started to arrive.

"All trees," said Mr. Coe, "are fruit trees." Mr. Coe said a lot of things that made no sense. "Unless someone has jiggered with them."

I thought he was done. But it was just a very long pause. "We don't want jiggered trees. Like flowering crabs and ornamental cherries. What is it we don't want?"

"Jiggered trees."

"And those are?"

"Trees that don't make fruit," seemed to be the appropriate response.

"Agreed. That would be fruitless."

He had a way of saying things like that without even a hint of a smile.

"What I've done is ordered two of everything for our little ark: pears, plums, peaches, cherries, lemons, oranges, bananas. And one big apple tree. A regular fruit salad—I see you have a question, Curtis?"

"We're going to grow bananas in New England?"

"I don't see why not. You like bananas, don't you?"

∝

I asked my parents about Mr. Coe. After all, they found me the summer job. They said Albert Coe had lived in the neighborhood longer than anybody, and all the neighbors thought highly of him. He kept up his place. Which was their way of saying he wasn't weird or anything. They figured he had just gotten too old to mow his own lawn and needed a little help. Which is what I thought when I showed up that first day. I had no clue. He didn't want me to mow the lawn. He wanted me to dig it all up. And plant a humongous garden as a gift for his invisible wife.

I didn't exactly tell the parents that. Just that he had a lot of gardening he wanted done. I didn't want them to think he was crazy. I figured he might be crazy, but nice-crazy. And you have to show that some respect.

☙

Midway through our fourth week of gardening I was digging in the center of the back yard and my shovel hit something solid. Definitely not a rock. Something metallic that rang like it was hollow inside.

"Mr. Coe, I think I found something buried in the garden."

"Ah! San Damiano!"

"Umm. Sure. Whatever." Mr. Coe was so old that he thought people knew stuff that actually nobody knows.

"See Curtis, when St. Francis moved out of his parent's house to begin his new life, the first thing he did was rebuild a tumbled-down chapel called San Damiano. He was starting from scratch. But he was young and enthusiastic, like Elizabeth and I were."

"There's a chapel buried in your back yard?"

"That would be imprecise. But fundamentally accurate."

There was no point rushing Mr. Coe. He wasn't going to make any more sense until he decided to.

"It used to be clearly marked," he said after another long pause. "With a ceramic statue of St. Francis. Until he was assassinated by some hired barbarian with a riding lawnmower."

I tapped whatever it was with the tip of my shovel. Definitely metal. I scraped away some soil and you could see a little glint of something silvery. Of course I wanted to dig it up. But Mr. Coe was in no hurry.

"Relics. Any chapel worth its salt had some sort of holy relics. The ones you're so eager to excavate are vintage 1962. Ancient by almost any calculation."

"But what *is* it?"

"It's a time capsule."

"A what?"

"A letter to the future. Back then we were really interested in the future. It was right around the corner. We imagined we would have solved all our problems by now. And our perfected world would be nostalgic for a glimpse of the old days," said Mr. Coe. "What we didn't count on was people losing interest in the future itself."

"So it's a box of stuff from 1962?"

"October to be exact. Just after Elizabeth and I moved into this house. Probably we should re-bury it."

"But," I said, "what if there's something *valuable* in there?"

"There is." Mr. Coe unrolled his Treasure Map and pointed to the part of the garden we were working on. We were standing where those pizza wedge paths all kind of came together right there in the middle. "Let's get back to planting somebody in this lacuna. When your shovel ran into the past, we were secretly plotting the fate of that big apple tree trussed up in burlap over there. A case of Malus aforethought. If you please, Mr. Curtis, some dynamite in the hole."

I raised my hand and waited out Mr. Coe. My hand was getting tired when he finally noticed it. "Curtis you appear to have a question. Might I infer that it's about the contents of that time capsule?"

I squeaked out some sort of answer. I guess I said the right thing because he put down the garden plan and told me the story.

"Elizabeth and I, that's Mrs. Coe, took possession of this domicile in August 1962. It was what they called a spec house, in the new split-level style. That was the spring of the Mercury astronauts. The summer of the Seattle World's Fair. The 'World of Tomorrow,' with the Space Needle and the Monorail. There was such pervasive enthusiasm for the Future then that the developer outfitted every new house sold with its own stainless steel time capsule.

"We were the pioneers, Elizabeth and I. The New Frontier. There were no lawns then, no stockade fences. Just a lot of scraped half-acre lots and construction sites as far as the eye could see. That was August.

"The world came to an end that October. They probably don't talk about the End of the World in high school history class—if they still teach history—but it happened. Nowadays it's been safely filed away as some dusty old episode called The Cuban Missile Crisis. Just another crisis among many. For us pre-Cambrian fossils who lived through it, it was anything but. Make no mistake; it was, to date, the most perilous incident in all of human history. That week before Halloween, sudden and certain Death stood on every man's doormat, his knuckles raised to knock.

"On October 22nd President Kennedy in black and white revealed to us a trail of irrefutable evidence that none of us even suspected. The hated Russians were behind a *secret, swift, and extraordinary buildup of Communist missiles* on the little isle of Cuba, just a stone's throw from Florida. Yes, he called them 'Communist missiles.' Then our president, who always seemed youthful, but suddenly seemed just too young, pronounced words that froze our blood: *We will not prematurely or unnecessarily risk the costs of worldwide nuclear war in which even the fruits of victory would be ashes in our mouth—but neither will we shrink from that risk.*

"When his address to the nation ended, we just had to turn the television off. In those days the screen didn't go black all at once. An intensely bright dot in the center of the screen glowed in the blackness, then slowly faded out. For six days we sat in our suburb waiting for the mushroom cloud.

"Many put their faith in canned goods. And ammunition. There was a run on grocery stores. Americans stood ready, prepared to gun down their next-door neighbors clawing like rabid dogs at the hatch to their shelter. To protect their stockpile of food. That's when that venomous weed got planted.

"But there was no time for us to dig a fallout shelter, and realistically that didn't make much sense. The term in and of itself was risible. Everyone knew what fallout was: atomic dust that stayed radioactive for hundreds of years and concentrated in the food chain. Hiding in a hole was no shelter from that. And with the Ruskies aiming ICBMs at us from Cuba there'd be no warning in any event. We'd already dug a small hole in the back yard, but that was for the Time Capsule. It was still sitting in what the realtor euphemistically called the "sewing room," (though it was called the Nursery on the blueprints), while we decided on what memorabilia to include for future archaeologists.

"Elizabeth and I stopped using the word 'tomorrow' that week. We couldn't leave each other's sight because we might never see each other again. We huddled in bed with the blankets drawn up to our noses, but we didn't sleep because you needed to be awake when it happened. We repeatedly switched the television on, then quickly off. *Leave It to Beaver* and the cheery jingles of the sponsors felt macabre to us. The news gave no relief. We felt like there was nothing we could do. Helpless. So we did something. We filled that metal capsule and buried it under a peaceful saint."

I tried to pry it up a bit with the tip of my shovel. The metal thing in the hole was still shiny, rounded like an elongated egg.

"Elizabeth. Curtis wants to know what's in the box," said Mr. Coe, though there was no Elizabeth there to talk to. Then he stood there for the longest time, like he was listening to someone. Then he goes: "Sorry son, it's not rare old coins or first edition comic books…."

Comics? Seriously? Like he thinks that's what I'm into?

Then he goes: "It wasn't a time for ephemera. We filled it with the one thing that we had. The one thing that we wanted to deliver to whatever future there might possibly be. We wrote down our love for each other. As a prayer against despair. We wrote down all of it, the whole history, not just the flowery parts. Each of us took a notebook and started with the day we met. We pledged complete honesty. No peeking. It took days. We were newlyweds, so naturally we felt like we had invented something." Mr. Coe broke off. "I think an apple tree is just the ticket."

"But we can't just bury it again. You know, the capsule thing."

"I suspect that after sixty years a Cortland apple tree would fructify better than a bunch of my jejune love notes."

I didn't know what "jejune" or "fructify" meant, but it sounded weird. Like a lot of little things, all of which had to do with Mrs. Coe. Mr. Coe said we were building this garden for her. But I'd never seen her. And I'd been inside the house, the kitchen at least, every day for lunch and she definitely wasn't in there. I totally had no clue where she was. I'm not even sure that Mr. Coe knew, and maybe hadn't for a long time. But he talked about her as if she would show up any day and catch us with the garden half-finished. And he wanted the garden done the first time she saw it. I mean, Mr. Coe wasn't Alzheimer crazy or anything, but maybe when you get really old you know more dead people than living ones. And you start to believe in ghosts. If I was building a garden for a dead lady, I felt like I oughtta know that. There was no way I could just ask if his wife was, you know, dead. But I kinda asked.

"Shouldn't Mrs. Coe get a vote too? Half of what's in the box is hers."

"A salient point, Curtis."

ICYMI, I need a dictionary app on my cell. But I doubt Mr. Coe would let me use it. He, like, never texts *anybody*. He has no clue what an emoji is. He thinks a phone is a *phone*; you know, for making voice calls.

"Mrs. Coe is sure to have her own perspective. She always has."

Anyway, we didn't plant the apple tree. He had me leave it there next to the time capsule hole. Bundled in burlap. Beside that big lacuna.

I wish I could say that things went smoothly after that. They didn't. The next day when I arrived Mr. Coe was pulling up all kinds of plants that we'd already planted. He was sweating. With stripes of dirt on his pants and big bunches of greenery in each fist. He was doing exactly what my parents told me I shouldn't let him do. Overexert himself.

"Curtis!" he called me over, "I've received a visitation from Clio."

So, who's Clio? His wife is named Elizabeth.

"She informs me we've been doing everything wrong. And you don't argue with a muse."

I did the long slow "'kaaay..." since I really had no idea why he was waving around bunches of flowers with dirt dripping off their roots.

"Not radiating spokes like some suburban Fontainebleau! One continuous sinuosity!"

I sat down on the bench in the middle of the garden and put my hands in my lap. My thought was that if I just kind of slowed it way down, got real chill, Mr. Coe would too. Before he busted something.

It worked. He sat down and let me take the uprooted perennials out of his hands. I went and got him a glass of iced tea from the fridge. He wiped his hands on an old towel. He put on his garden gloves and had me bring out the snakes. And that big wooden circus tent hammer. And we worked together like usual with him doing most of the talking and me doing almost all the digging.

It took us the rest of the week, but we put the garden back together according to Mr. Coe's new Treasure Map 2.0. Hopefully this was a stable version.

A few days after that Mr. Coe made a big announcement. As usual, he started out by saying something I couldn't make sense of.

"Today is a Red Letter Day," said Mr. Coe.

"Right. OK," I said. And I was thinking he's somewhere back in the day when people still sent letters. With, you know, stamps.

"Mrs. Coe is coming home today."

That I wasn't expecting. "What?"

"Today. I know, the garden's not finished, but there it is."

I had to ask. "Where has she been?"

Mr. Coe went into another one of his long silences. I started to wonder if he had heard me, though there was nothing wrong with his hearing. I was about to ask again, then I thought, maybe it's a bad question. I'd never seen Mr. Coe mad about anything, but when he finally answered me, the word sounded angry.

"Hospice."

"The hospital?"

"The diametrical opposite. Hospital is where you go to get better. Hospice is where you go to get worse."

I didn't know what to say to that. So I started cleaning up the garden, putting away tools, and sacks of "dynamite" for when Mrs. Coe showed up. He stood in the middle of the garden we'd created, unmoving, like he was the statue of St Francis, or whoever. I started to ask him where he wanted me to put something. Then I saw a tear on his cheek. Just one. Then he started talking, like into the air.

"She flunked out. Just like I told her she would. When the oncologist said he'd emptied his bag of tricks, I told her to come home. I'd take care of her. Biggest argument we ever had. She had her own perspective. Hospice."

I tried to say something nice. "They must have taken good care of her. Now, you can welcome her home."

"Curtis," said Mr. Coe, and his voice sounded like it had a little bit of a smile in it. And then he didn't say anything.

We tried to get back to work on the garden, but Mr. Coe was distracted. He had me move things around and then move them back where I had found them. I think he was trying to make it look finished when it obviously wasn't. He didn't know how to do that. I didn't either.

That afternoon a car pulled up in front of the house and someone rang the doorbell. Mr. Coe stripped off his gardening gloves, sighed, and went into the house to answer the door. I looked in through the kitchen window.

Elizabeth Coe looked nothing like I expected. For one thing, she was completely bald. Mr. Coe made up for his whisps of hair with big brushy eyebrows. I'm pretty sure Mrs. Coe had no eyebrows at all. She held out a hand to Mr. Coe. He kind of stood there, like he didn't know what to do. It was like watching a movie, except in a movie something major would have happened next.

What happened next was a guy with a clipboard came in behind Mrs. Coe and wanted her husband to sign. Like she was a FedEx package.

So, he signed. And the hospice delivery guy noticed me staring at the bald woman through the back window and gave me a "say, hey" gesture. Embarrassing.

"Curtis," said Mr. Coe, "Come in here. I'd like you to meet Mrs. Coe."

I went in through the kitchen door to where they were standing by the front door and shook hands. "Elizabeth Coe," she said, like very polite. And gave me the steady gaze of someone who has no idea who you are or what you're doing there. Her hand was so bony it was like a Halloween handshake, but her grip was firm as steel.

The delivery guy clipped his pen back into his top pocket and kind of backed out the front door.

"Curtis here is helping me with a little project," said Mr. Coe, like he didn't want to say too much. But she'd already looked past me through the kitchen to the backyard beyond.

"Albert," said Mrs. Coe, "what exactly has been going on around here while I was gone?"

"I—we—have been building a garden," he said. "Come and see."

So, Albert Coe took Elizabeth's hand and led her across the old kitchen and out through the backyard door. I followed behind.

"This isn't a garden," she said.

"Well, it isn't finished, dear."

"No, I mean it's the whole back yard. A garden is a bed of flowers. This is more like an arboretum. Or a botanical exhibition."

This wasn't like what Mr. Coe was looking for. He went into another one of his long silences. So I went and sat down on the wheelbarrow over by the sacks of dynamite. To, you know, be out of the middle of it. I pulled out my cell phone. Usually, Mr. Coe would admonish me to Be Here Now. But I figured he wouldn't this time. I went into my social apps. But after about a millisecond of looking at selfies of people I barely knew, I kinda stopped looking at the screen. My fingers kept paging and swiping and liking. But what I was doing was listening.

"Dear, let me show you. This isn't just something decorative. This is our private garden," goes Mr. Coe.

"It used to be our private back lawn."

"Granted," said Mr. Coe, "but isn't this better?"

"It's obviously kept you busy."

"I had to do something. What with you ignoring all my entreaties and traipsing off to…"

"Let's not." said Mrs. Coe. "So you built an enormous garden. Without telling me. Were you planning to surprise me?"

"Well, you do seem to be surprised."

Mrs. Coe walked around the garden, leaning hard on this weird cane with, like, feet. She wasn't looking at the plants. She was shaking her head like it was full of things to say rushing off in all directions and crowding each other out. So full that, like, none of those words could beat out the others to get spoken. At the exact same time she looked like she was waiting for Mr. Coe to say something. Women are like that. I don't know what he was supposed to say, but he didn't say it.

"OK, I suppose I have to answer my own question," said Mrs. Coe. "Clearly, you've been working on this project for weeks, if not months. So you must have started it when there was about zero chance that I would ever leave Hospice. If I had taken the morphine primrose path they offered me, I certainly wouldn't have."

"You went there to die."

"No, Albert. That's what I was trying to explain to you, and you just wouldn't get it. I went there to fight. In the hospice I could scream out my rage and pain. And nobody would care much. I couldn't do that, Albert, if you'd been there nursing me. You would have been terrified. You'd want to do something to make it better. And then I'd be taking care of you.

"It wasn't a good bet that I was going to get better. But for certain it wasn't going to get better with soothing.

"Neither of us are children. People who beat cancer don't do it because they fight harder. The cancer is you. It's you eating you up from within, like a snake swallowing its own tail. But I was determined not to go gentle into that good night. F that. I prayed. I didn't pray for miraculous healing. That's for amateurs. I prayed to be preserved from despair. I prayed and I cursed, and I didn't give up. And maybe, just maybe, that gave my body the time to stop making the cancer. I don't understand remission. What I do understand is permission, and I was determined to give that to my raging bodily self, regardless of how much agony it was going to repay me in return.

"And then a week ago I woke up to something other than pain. It was weird, like waking up with a numb hand. There was nothing exultant about it. It was strangely calm, unfamiliar and yet deeply familiar. Déjà vu. Hospice isn't really equipped for diagnosis. But I had the phone number of my oncologist, and he took my call. And when I said 'Dr. Caldwell, I think I'm in remission' he took me seriously enough to ask some questions. And here I am."

Mr. Coe finally spoke. He goes: "I love you, Elizabeth." I think he said the right thing. Mrs. Coe kind of ran over to him, if you can imagine a really really old, completely bald woman running with a cane. They did this big hug thing. I kept my eyes glued to my cell screen.

After a long time, Mrs. Coe stepped back about an arm's length. She was holding Mr. Coe's hands in her totally bony ones and gazing into his eyes.

"So where were you going to put the ashes?" she said.

"Right over there, center of the garden, at the base of that apple tree."

"Sweet," she said.

They sat down together on the bench in Mr. Coe's garden. That cane stood up all by itself. They were quiet for a while. I think they had forgotten I was even there.

"Don't sit under the apple tree with anybody else but me," said Mrs. Coe.

"If you love me, if you really love me, plant a rose for me. If you're going to love me for a long, long time, plant an apple tree," said Mr. Coe. They were rhyming, like they were, you know, rapping to each other. And then they were laughing.

"Curtis," called out Mr. Coe. "Be so kind as to tell Mrs. Coe what you dug up here in the epicenter of our garden."

"Um," I said, "it was sort of a time capsule. I didn't open it. Promise."

"You remember the shattered St. Francis?" he said, turning to Mrs. Coe.

"Like it was yesterday," said Mrs. Coe.

"That's where we're going to plant the apple tree. Of course you can see we haven't quite planted it, yet. But there it is."

Mrs. Coe then started talking to me. "Curtis, I assume you live around here."

"Just a couple of blocks over. With my parents. The Robinet's."

"And you're in high school?"

"Just finished my sophomore year."

"And in the fall?"

"Well, there's school. And I'm trying out for Varsity Track."

"So you won't be around to keep up this enormous garden?"

I didn't quite know what to say to that.

"Albert is going to need a whole landscaping crew to weed and water, fertilize and prune this quarter acre of hothouse plants. But naturally he didn't think of that. I've always had to be the practical one."

I wanted to say to her that Mr. Coe was plenty practical. He'd planned out this whole garden from just nothing. Drew it all out on paper. Most people couldn't do that, even people who aren't, like, super old. And he figured out how to get all the plants and the dynamite, and everything else.

But Mr. Coe didn't do a thing to defend himself. His smile just got wider and wider at what she said. It was like this put-down was making him, I don't know, happy?

"Mr. Coe," I said, "Show her how you planned all this out, figured out all the measurements and everything."

"She doesn't need to involve herself with all that, Curtis."

I felt like Mrs. Coe should know just how amazing Mr. Coe was. "No, seriously, show her the Treasure Map."

"Is this it?" said Mrs. Coe, picking up the big roll of paper leaning against the bench. She unscrolled it and began reading aloud:

"'Syringa,' 'Rosa rugosa,' 'First Meeting: McMannis Boathouse';
'Forsythia,' 'She taught me to rollerskate (hopeless)'; 'Delphnium,'
'Polygonatum,' 'Proposal of Marriage'... Oh, Albert."

"That's why," said Mr. Coe, "the garden had to be so big."

"Albert," said Elizabeth Coe, and tears started to run down out
of her eyes. "Are you sure that it's begun?"

"I used to be able to bring things back by going through the alphabet. In the last few weeks, I've started to lose track of the alphabet
halfway through. Good days and bad days. I never knew that the letter Z could make me so inordinately happy."

"So this is your memory garden," said Mrs. Coe.

"A garden of *our* memories. With the old direct paths breaking
down I had to find a new way to bring them back. A new encoding.
Sinuosity. A path among flowers, shapes and colors. They say the
olfactory sense is the most retentive." said Mr. Coe.

I'm just telling you what they said. Most of it didn't make a lot
of sense to me. But it was like a private moment. I didn't want to be
there listening to it. But I was like there, listening to it.

"You went off to Hospice. And I began to forget. I thought *if
there was a garden. And a path in it to walk. And an apple tree...* And
then Curtis here helped me build it. Because you were gone. And I
couldn't." said Mr. Coe, "I couldn't bear to lose you twice."

Vacation

Chapter 1

Having conclusively proved the existence of God, the theologian Thomas Kemp found himself with time on his hands. So he and his wife Grace decided to go on vacation.

The conclusions of Kemp's Proof of God's Existence are straightforward enough for anyone to grasp:

- There is something rather than nothing.
- The very existence of something requires consciousness.
- Consciousness is not possible without the inseparable essences of love, goodness, and beauty.

This simplicity does not mean that the road to its realization was easy. It took years to formulate.

Had he been a better theologian he never would have gotten there. That's not critique; it's the first sentence of Thomas's landmark book that laid out his Proof. Twenty-six pages that are, to date, irrefutable. His point was that a better theologian would have started from the arguments of generations of brilliant divines and logicians. Kemp didn't. His starting points were two recent scientific observations. One was a photograph from the Space Telescope that showed countless galaxies at a time in the early universe when galaxies

31

should not have existed. The other was an obscure behavioral phys-
iology paper on the morality of bees.

Now, about that vacation. Grace Kemp wanted to go to the
Grand Canyon. Not just to stand there and look down. It was her
desire to ride saddleback down the Bright Angel Trail into the heart
of the canyon. Given their ages, she felt that it was now or never to
make that descent. To have on one side of her the rocky strata of
uncountable eons of time. On the other side the thin air of the abyss.
Balanced in between on the conscious free will of a mule. She is, of
course, the wife of a theologian.

"I like horses. I trust them. They have horse sense. Frankly,
Thomas, I can't think of any other animal to which we attribute sen-
sibleness. There's a reason for that."

"But the beasts we'd be riding are mules. Their attribute is stubbornness." Thomas continued slicing onions. Dinner was gently
sautéing on the gas range. In half an hour they'd be eating his new
recipe. Grace loved his cooking, but got hungry and impatient
around this time, which made her metaphysical. Whatever project
or plan she had been formulating started to be presented as not only
a good idea, but a morally necessary one. A capstone, a resolution of
unresolved problems that Thomas was somehow utterly unaware of.

"The Bright Angel Trail," said Grace. "Think what that would
mean to Rafe. And to the girls. That we'd been on the Bright Angel
Trail."

The onions sizzling with other ingredients in the pan, Thomas
had moved on to dicing summer squash. "Absolutely," he said. He
was trying to piece together the connection his wife had already
made between their hypothetical trip into the Grand Canyon and

the putative good effects of hearing about it afterwards on their three grown children. Grace slid around him at the kitchen counter, giving him a squeeze from behind in passing. He knew where she was going.

"It's not done yet."

Grace was already holding the spoon, cooling it with her breath. "Did you know," she said, "that there's an Indian village at the bottom of the canyon. They've been there forever. Down by the river. They look up at those looming canyon walls, but they never go up there. Everything they need they either already have down there, or it comes down the trail in saddlebags."

"Panniers. I think the things mules wear are called panniers."

"I think we need to go there. To meet those people living authentic lives at the bottom of time."

"They sell stuff to tourists."

"Thomas, what's in this? It's delicious."

"An absence of summer squash, mostly."

"No. I mean the spice. You're such a good cook."

"It's a balancing act. There's the warm spices: cumin, cinnamon, the usual suspects. But then there's something no one expects."

"The Spanish Inquisition?"

Thomas smiled. He would follow Grace anywhere, even into a gouge in the earth to buy vastly overpriced Native American basketry. "Nope. Thyme. Just a little bit of thyme."

ɞ

Thomas had accepted the invitation to lecture at Northern Arizona University mostly due to the proximity of the campus to the Grand Canyon. The Kemps, after all, were on vacation. As they got on the plane to Flagstaff he asked Grace if the office would miss her. "I can work from anywhere," she replied. Thomas clicked his seatbelt and said he could top that. "These days," he said, "I can work from Nowhere."

The plane climbed into the air and carried them west.

"Horseback I can envision," said Thomas. "But mules?"

"You're thinking about mules all wrong. Sure, they're a cross between a donkey and a horse," said Grace. "But that doesn't mean they're half-assed horses. In fact, they're noble beasts, closer in intelligence and temperament to horses, but more steadfast, less skittish. And surprisingly social. I think that comes from the fact that they don't breed—at least not successfully."

"As opposed to us, who have been quite successful at it?"

Grace smiled, "We've had a pretty good run."

Thomas leaned close in his airplane seat and whispered, "Much as I know this horsewoman don't approve of spurs," he winked, "I'm not ready to hang up mine."

"Getting back to mules," said Grace, "Every once in a while, they do breed successfully. Kind of a miracle. Grist for your theological mill."

"Is that what those Bethlehem shepherds were coming to the stable to see?"

"Oh, you are a wicked Catholic!" Grace slapped him playfully.

"I'm going to Arizona to talk to a room full of astronomers about God. That will be my penance."

೦೩

Arriving early at the university, Grace took a seat in the middle of the empty lecture hall and returned corporate emails as the room slowly filled with graduate students and faculty.

Laying out Kemp's Proof took Thomas all of twenty minutes. He started at the Beginning: The Big Bang. And didn't mention God. He could feel this making the audience nervous. Everyone wanted a theologian to put God back at the first instant of time. If He's not there at the Beginning, letting there be light, what kind of a God is He? But at that timeless non-time, existence and non-existence were exactly the same thing. If you've got no time and no space, then nothing matters.

He moved on. Of course, he knew there would be more Big Bang arguments coming in the Q & A. NAU was notoriously full of astronomers.

Nope, Kemp's Proof pivoted on a later, greater mystery. God exists outside of time but acts within it. And once you've got time, pretty soon you've got matter. And antimatter.

For every created particle of matter there is—there must be—an equal and opposite created particle of antimatter. Antimatter and matter should pair off exactly, particle-for-particle, and continuously annihilate each other in a burst of light. But. There's Something rather than Nothing because—God knows—they don't. There's vastly more matter than antimatter, regardless of where we look. This huge, mysterious imbalance has been known for a hundred years: it's called baryon asymmetry, for those who need fancy terminology. And no scientist can account for it. It is why you, me—and everything else—exist.

Thomas could feel the audience shift uncomfortably in their seats. He had them now. After a pause, he continued his lecture.

"Then," he said, "in a cosmological blink of an eye you've got galaxies. Not only matter, but *structured* matter. Thanks to the Space Telescope we've now got the photos. Galaxies much sooner than every theory's cosmic timepiece says is possible. Just as if they were being *created*." Thomas refrained from adding "and it was good." No sense poking the bear.

He looked out at Grace in the middle row. She flashed him an encouraging smile. He went on to the next point.

Plenty was happening, all right. And for the quantum mechanics in the audience that was a breakdown that they couldn't fix. Occurrence requires consciousness, the spooky Schrödinger's cat notion that an observer is required to collapse potentiality to actuality. Kemp posed a *reductio ad absurdum*: "When I die does the universe cease to exist? No? OK. How about if all of us perish, *then* does the universe cease to exist?" He let the question hang out there. That kind of Consciousness was necessary, but not sufficient, for any Deity that Thomas would care to know. Divine Consciousness requires benevolent engagement.

Thomas turned to the third leg of the Proof: love, goodness, and beauty. Essences immanent from God and inherent to all life, so interdependent that Kemp refers to them by a single name: LoGo B. He cited a journal article about honeybees. And he offered a simple human formulation: *We love what is good; what we love is beautiful to us.* "Sorry Keats," he added, "no Truth."

After that, Thomas spent the rest of his standard lecture on the "making of" documentary. He quoted Nicholas of Cusa, who would have been a sure crowd-pleaser among the astronomers, had they ever heard of him. A hundred years before Copernicus he'd already thrown out the whole structure of a fixed Earth at the center of a cosmos of perfect crystalline spheres. And got away with it. According to Nicholas of Cusa, there is no center, and everything is moving relative to everything else. He was an amazingly good cosmologist, but Bishop Nicholas was an even better theologian: *God is a sphere of which the center is everywhere and the circumference nowhere.* Pretty good definition of an immanent and omnipresent God. Pretty good definition of the universe.

You kind of know what's coming by the quality of the applause. This crowd's clapping sounded respectful, if a bit baffled. There was a widespread acceptance that they'd heard something to ponder. That they couldn't write it off as sleight of hand. As in any audience, there were plenty who felt sure that they could find the fatal flaw. But they pretty much knew they weren't going to find it in the next half hour. A proof of the existence of God? Food for thought, at least.

There was an astonishingly tall young man in the first row who didn't clap at all. As soon as Thomas stepped to the podium his glance had been drawn irresistibly to this student. This fellow had to be in the front row. There was just no way his legs would have fit in any of the seating ranks behind him. Even slouched down with his limbs splayed out he was easily over seven feet tall. Not freakishly elongated, just built to a proportionately much larger template. As he lectured, Thomas had the absurd thought that if he somehow hadn't noticed this man's extreme height, this guy would easily count as the most non-descript person in the room.

Of course, the giant raised his hand for the first question. Except it wasn't quite a question.

"I miss faith," he said.

The whole lecture hall went silent. It wasn't a question or a counter-argument. Though it was stated calmly, it was an accusation.

"So do I," said Thomas Kemp.

At that point an overheated graduate student in the back of the room threw out the topic of Dark Matter, which—he made sure everyone was aware—makes up fully 85% of Everything. Flinging the question at the lecturer in a smug "bet you haven't thought of that" tone. Thomas took some time to explain how he found immense comfort in knowing that something exists without anyone understanding it.

When his gaze turned back to the front row, the seat was empty. It was hard to believe that he didn't see a seven-foot-tall man stand up and leave. But he didn't.

જી

You can see mountains a long distance away. Cities give themselves away by the light they cast on the horizon. On the open sea one can navigate to an island by observing the banked clouds above it. But nothing prepares you for the Grand Canyon. You have no way of knowing it's there until you are there.

Its arrival is so sudden and extreme that you can imagine the inattentive pitching over the edge. Conestoga. Pony Express. Model T. Following one after another over the canyon rim to plummet nearly a mile down. Falling would take a full twenty seconds. The sound of impact would take another five seconds to rebound to the top of the canyon.

Thomas and Grace stood at the South Rim Scenic Overlook and looked over.

"Wow," said a man who's on a first-name basis with God.

Grace started snapping photos. Then she stopped. "This is impossible. No way to capture even a hint of this." She looked at the images she'd just made on her cell phone, then started to erase them, one after another. "It's actually an insult to the place to try to take its photo." She looked about her at dozens of visitors wholly engaged in insulting the Grand Canyon.

"The thing is," said Thomas, "these folks are adding layer upon layer of images between us and the thing itself. If we believe in immanence—and I do—God and all His LoGo B qualities exist equally in any direct encounter with the created world. A clover, a speck of lint."

A man suddenly shouts. A dozen digital panoramas are interrupted as tourists turn to see what happened. Nothing happened. The man shrugs. He was hoping for an echo, but there's no hope of a voice returning from the far canyon wall across this vastness.

"These folks aren't going to find God in an echo. Or the image of a thing," said Thomas. "They have to be here, now."

"Dryer lint?" said Grace. "You're especially Zen today. Are you about to cite your favorite theologian?"

"No man is a prophet in his own laundry room. Guilty as charged. Theodor Seuss Geisel *Horton Hears a Who*."

"A person's a person, no matter how small," they recite together. Thomas walks his arm around Grace's waist. They stand together in silence at the South Rim Scenic Overlook as clouds scud across the brightness of the day.

 са

Back in the foyer of the Canyon Lodge a DVD of the vista a quarter mile away was playing again and again in endless loop. The season changed every three minutes, foreground snow succeeded by cactus flowers against the eternal palette of geological time. A plastic box was propped against a corner of the overhead screen, making it clear that you could take this memory home with you. Available in the gift shop.

Thomas was resting his feet in a chair made of discarded antlers. Grace was talking to the receptionist at the concierge desk, a well-dressed much younger woman. Who was polite, but unambiguous. "There's no Kemp here."

"That's Thomas and Grace Kemp. K-E-M-P. It has to be there. We phoned over two months ago to make the canyon descent reservation. We sent in the forms. They said we were all set."

"I'm very sorry, ma'am. There's simply nothing here."

Grace winced at the word "ma'am". "Thomas Kemp," she said. "That's my husband over there. Surely you've heard of Thomas Kemp. The writer."

The word "writer" always got a better response than theologian or philosopher. But not this time. The woman at the desk didn't even glance at the supposed famous writer.

"We're booked solid. I could put you on the standby list. But it could be days before there's a cancellation and two mules become available. You'll have to check in at 5:30am, in person, every morning. If you'd like me to add you to the list…"

Back in their Canyon Lodge room, Grace tried to phone the Phantom Ranch. At the end of their long mulish descent, they were supposed to spend the night in a rustic fieldstone cabin at Phantom Ranch. Thomas was unimpressed with photos of the cabins. He felt the mules got the better accommodations. Grace reminded him how hard reservations were to get. And pointed out that the cabins, along with nearly every other building at the Grand Canyon, were designed by Mary Jane Colter, America's first female professional architect.

Surely if Grace could prove to the concierge at the front desk that there was a room awaiting them at Phantom Ranch, they'd have to find the mules to get them there.

But getting a cell phone connection to Phantom Ranch proved elusive. After the fourth "hello?" followed by loss of signal, Thomas was tempted to comment on the "phantom" part of the name. He had always found humor a way to cope with exasperation. Grace didn't. After thirty years of marriage, he finally knew enough to keep his mouth shut.

"Maybe the connection problem is on our end," said Thomas. "You know, all these Lincoln Log walls. Let's go out to the front porch and try from there."

"Maybe we could get some coffee in the lobby?"

"That's the spirit," said Thomas. Cowboy coffee might be just what was needed. That, and prayer.

In theory, Kemp's Proof had no specific role for prayer. The conscious presence of a beneficent God was baked into the very existence of everything. Being conscious and immanent in time meant that divine ripples continually coursed through existence in answering echoes to human consciousness. And any other kind of consciousness.

In practice, Thomas subscribed to the God of the Medium-sized Hardware Store: Big enough to have everything you need, small enough to take a personal interest in you.

Out on the porch of the hotel, outside of the huge timbers that framed the building, they put down their paper coffee cups and tried again. Grace punched the number for Phantom Ranch into her cell phone. Thomas hovered nearby making helpful hand motions, like a baseball fan gesturing a long ball into the bleachers. They both heard the ringing of the distant Phantom Ranch desk phone echoing in Grace's hand.

Someone walked past them and entered the hotel. Someone at least seven feet tall. Thomas caught only a glimpse as the man ducked his head to enter through the undersized front door. Again, he had the sense that this was not a basketball player, not someone afflicted by Marfan syndrome or gigantism, not a freak of nature. All was proportional. The most natural thing in the world. Thomas couldn't testify that it was the same man from the lecture hall. He seemed older. He could have been thirty. Or fifty. But honestly, how many men that size were likely to be walking around Northern Arizona?

"Hello?" said Grace, "Phantom Ranch? Yes. I'm calling about a reservation for Kemp. Grace and Thomas Kemp. Yes. For this week…"

"Thomas, write this down." He found a pen in one pocket and a scrap of paper in another. She dictated the reservation number, and he wrote it down. "Got it."

"Let me read that back to you," said Grace. "47… hello? Hello? Phantom Ranch, it seems I've lost you. If you can still hear me, thank you. We'll be seeing you soon."

Grace was exultant. "There's more than one way to skin a mule!" She was ready to march back to that concierge desk holding high irrefutable proof of the existence of their reservation.

But all that was in Thomas's mind was the urge to say "Did you see that?" But the moment had passed, and it would be too complicated to explain. So he said nothing about the seven foot man. Instead, he spoke without thinking. "So much for no record of the Kemps! That young woman is about to learn that stubbornness isn't an attribute unique to mules."

"Not stubbornness, dear. I'd hate to be thought of as stubborn. Just persistent. When we know we're right."

"Right."

They re-entered the foyer together, paper coffee cups in hand, ready to prove their case. But the foyer was empty. Not a soul in sight. Marching to the concierge desk, Grace rang the little bell that was supposed to summon help. Its tinny echo only confirmed that the Kemps were quite alone. Grace peered around the reception desk, hoping to find the clerk hiding down on her hands and knees.

"He was just here," said Thomas Kemp.

"Pronouns, Thomas. The only receptionist I've seen is a she. Though as a wife it's reassuring that you didn't notice."

"Not her. The tall guy."

"Tall?"

"Well over seven feet. Brobdingnagian. You must have seen him."

"There's a really, really tall receptionist?"

"No, he just walked in here. While we were outside."

"Well, he's not behind the desk. Or beneath it." Grace gave the hand bell another ineffectual tap.

On the overhead screen summer turned to autumn turned to winter. After a few more seasons, the concierge finally appeared through a swinging side door. Clicking across the tiled foyer floor, she held her hands out in front of her, dripping wet.

"Sorry," she said. "They're out of paper towels. Again."

Grace laid her scrap of paper out on the countertop, spreading it flat with her hands, presenting her proof. The concierge stared at the reservation number, then at her keyboard, then at her hands. Finally, with the Sigh of Sacrifice, she wiped her hands on the front of her skirt. In a few moments, which seemed endless to Grace, the computer coughed up the Bright Angel Trail Descent reservation for Tom Camp.

"Oops," said the receptionist, noting the typo.

"Nobody calls him 'Tom'," said Grace.

"Whatever." The girl squinted at the screen. "Anyway, this does appear to be your reservation. Day after tomorrow."

"Where do we meet our mules?" said Thomas.

"Umm," said the receptionist.

She turned back to her computer and started clicking furiously. Then she pulled a paper folder from a shelf behind the desk and paged through it. Back at the keyboard she clicked some more.

"Unfortunately," said the receptionist.

It turned out that Tom Camp and Party failed to show up to fill out their Waivers of Liability. Without a signed and recorded advance waiver, Park Service regulations would not allow trail access. Bright Angel Tours had no choice but to reassign the mounts.

"You gave away our mules?" Grace ejaculated. Thomas knew that when Grace started down this road things could get personal really fast. He knew he had to intervene. He laid a calming hand atop Grace's on the counter. He could feel her quivering.

"They're mules," he said. "I bet you have a lot of mules. If you could just make a phone call to add two more..."

"Sir. This is not an amusement park ride." It had been her last chance to avert what was coming. And she didn't take it. Either the girl hugely underestimated Grace, or she believed that being younger and on the right side of the desk gave her some kind of advantage. Thomas knew better.

"Who died," said Grace Kemp "and made you queen?"

"Excuse me?"

"You will not. I repeat. Not. Speak to my husband that way."

"Ma'am. If you're going to adopt that attitude."

"I think you've done all the adopting already. The attitude orphanage is empty. Your majesty."

The young receptionist clammed up. She tried to act as if Grace wasn't there. As if she was free to catch up on paperwork. As if Grace were a high desert rainstorm that would pass in a moment, leaving the air freshened. And empty.

"Silence," said Grace Kemp. "Right. I must say it suits you. Since not a word you've spoken has contained an ounce of compassion or remorse. Or willingness to help. I thought this was the Help Desk. I see I was misinformed." Grace was just getting started. But she stopped and looked up. Way, way up. At the seven-foot gentleman who quietly slipped behind the counter.

"May I solve a problem here?" he said. The young receptionist took the opportunity to make herself scarce.

❧

The Morality of Bees

Like many classic experiments, this one is simple in outline and incredibly detailed in execution. Start with a hive of honeybees. Fill up a flatbed truck with potted plants in flower. Park the truck in a hay field. Then wait. Eventually one scout bee from the hive finds the flowers. She returns to the hive to announce her discovery.

A scout bee reports the direction, distance, and quality of a source of nectar by performing an elaborate waggle dance deep within the hive, surrounded by worker bees [Von Frisch, 1967; Riley et al., 2005]. The workers interpret the danced directions, smell the nectar on the scout, and make a beeline to the source.

Then you drive the truck away.

When the worker bees arrive, there are no flowers. None. The workers are baffled. Puzzled, they enlarge their search area, compensate for wind. Still nothing. The scout has lied to them, apparently.

The heart of the experiment is to observe very closely the interaction between the scout and the workers when they return empty to the hive. To observe the morality of bees.

If these were theoretical bees, mechanical bees, their inescapable conclusion would be that the scout bee was defective. She would be replaced by a more reliable unit. Questions about deceit and trust, honor, forgiveness, or the lack of forgiveness would not enter in. But they do.

Put the truck back. Wait for the scout to return. For the scout will return to prove her truthfulness. Watch her flit among the flowers, watch her beeline back to the hive. Move the truck.

Before you go back to the hive to watch what happens, observe yourself. You feel terrible. There's such sympathy for this poor scout bee who is telling the truth and not being believed. By moving the truck, you are doing something that seems so indelibly wrong that it feels like a sin.

Meanwhile, back at the hive, the highly structured formalized world of the bees is falling apart. No mechanistic instinct holds sway, since in the world of bees whole fields of flowers don't move. Viewing the worker bees as a unit, their response seems chaotic; looking at the workers individually, their responses seem familiar. These are the experimental results. And there is no neat conclusion. Except, significantly, that there is no neat conclusion.

What rules the behavior of bees is a collective hive mind. The assumption has been that individual bees don't have individual consciousness. Except they do [Perry, Baciadonna, and Chittka, 2016]. When you move a field of flowers, the bees have no single communal reaction. Their responses splinter off in a dozen directions, depending on the individual. Responses that are unpredictable, but not random.

How they behave rests on something more fundamental than instinct.

Humans talk about a higher consciousness, a higher moral sense overlaid on a primitive reptilian brain of brute instinct. But what if consciousness of goodness, love, beauty is in fact a *lower* consciousness, something more inherent and fundamental to being alive that exists *beneath* instincts?

Go beneath the instincts of bees to find that truthfulness and lying, faith and doubt, punishment and forgiveness all enter in. Anthropomorphized constructs, certainly. But in whatever honeybee form they exist, they engage a world of moral consciousness, a connection to Divine Consciousness that is inherent to what it is to be alive. LoGo B. A piece of Kemp's Proof of God's Existence.

୧୨

"May I help you?" said the tall man. He was dressed entirely in beige: light khaki pants, starched shirt, and a taupe tie that looked like a clip-on.

Grace craned her neck up from the buttons of his shirt to look at his face. "Please," she said.

Once apprised of their situation the lofty concierge responded. Though he would feel so much happiness in adding mules for the Kemps, this would not be a good thing. It is the mules who bear the burden of the trek. It is hard on the mules. They must be rested between journeys down the canyon, restored physically and mentally for the safety of all. Each mule must be checked out by a veterinarian before being allowed on the trail. Certain mules get along better with certain other mules. Once on the trail, the trip leader can oversee only so many mounts and riders. Adding two more at the end of the string? They would be unsupervised. Which is never a good thing with mules. Bright Angel Tours could not vouch for their descent experience.

Grace took all this in. Thomas could see that she was about to insist. She didn't have to.

"However," said the clerk, "You do have valid reservations. A way must be found."

He sat down at the receptionist's computer like a visitor to a kindergarten class. His enormous hands hovering over the keys, an organist beginning a prelude. Just before his fingers descended, he turned to the Kemps with a wink of his eye and a twist of his head.

"This may take a little time," he said, "and you have already spent too much of your vacation standing in a lobby. I have your cell phone number. I will call soon. When I call, I will have good news. Rest assured that I would never call you with anything other than good news."

Thomas watched the seven-foot man wholly absorbed in his task. Was this the same guy slouched in the lecture hall? Was it even the same man he glimpsed entering the lodge? The clothing was different. But he could, of course, have changed into his work attire. Aside from their extreme height and a certain indeterminacy of age, there was nothing to distinguish them. They were non-descript. One man or three, they were wholly forgettable. If you could ever forget an encounter with a giant.

Ꮳ

Thomas had purchased a book at the gift shop: *A Field Guide to Geologic Time.* They were back at the South Rim Overlook, and he was paging back and forth, trying to identify the strata of rock and the extinct creatures whose fossilized bones were entombed in them. Grace was leaning perilously close to the railing, trying to chart the course of the Bright Angel Trail as it proceeded by innumerable switchbacks down the face of the canyon. Her cell phone began to ring. She didn't recognize the number.

"Hello?" she said.

"Good news," said the voice on the other end.

Though the voice was sunny, what he said didn't sound much like good news. He began by telling Grace Kemp that President Theodore Roosevelt came to the Grand Canyon in 1903. He met two members of the Havasupai tribe living there: Yavñmi' Gswedva, and a man we know only as Billy Burro. Teddy told them in ringing tones that this magnificent place would be declared a national park. Its beauty and majesty protected forever. Its splendor eternally undiminished. And that they would have to leave.

The last Havasupai were removed from the newly-created Grand Canyon National Park in 1928. The tribe by that time was nearly obliterated by imported diseases. Less than two hundred survived. Nevertheless, they persisted. In 1975 a bill was dragged reluctantly through Congress that returned some traditional usage rights. Rights that straddle the gray area between Federal regulation and Tribal rights. The right to perform religious ceremonies on Park Service land. The right to resupply the Havasupai village at the bottom of the canyon from the South Rim. Using their own pack mules.

"So we are to ride cargo hinnies down the canyon?" said Grace skeptically, "with panniers?"

"That would hardly be the good news I promised you. Yes, the Tribe maintains a small string of mules at the top of the canyon. But resupply by boat is cheaper and easier, so they almost never use them.

"The tribe has no need of their mules," the voice continued. "But should they give them up, they would have no way to re-establish the privilege on Park Service land. So the Havasupai must maintain useless mules to retain their ancestral right."

"Even better," said Grace. "What you're proposing is we ride down the canyon on idle Native American mules who don't know the way?"

"That would be unwise," said the voice. "Here's the good news. The Havasupai get the money to maintain their corral rights by franchising their tribal concession to Vasari Corridor Tours. Vasari mules are experienced and extremely well-trained."

"So there's a second mule tour company?"

"No, actually there's not," said the voice. "I need to be very clear on that. The Park Service contracts Bright Angel Tours with exclusive rights to organize and promote canyon mule treks. But mules carry three things down the canyon trail: Tourists. On rare occasions, Tribal supplies. And celebrities. Vasari Tours exists to transport celebrities. The good news is that you have suddenly become movie stars.

"To the rest of the world, Vasari Tours does not exist. It does not, cannot, advertise, promote, or in any way infringe on the exclusive license of Bright Angel Tours. But people too famous to be seen with a pack of mule-riding tourists find a way to find Vasari. You are now those people."

The voice on the phone supplied the Kemps with the time and directions where they would meet up with their mules. Their deposit would be discreetly transferred from Bright Angel Tours to Vasari. In token of their inconvenience, there would be no additional charges. Grace bubbled over with gratitude for saving their vacation.

"One last thing," said the voice on the phone. "This call didn't happen."

಄

The next morning Thomas was up early at the Canyon Lodge breakfast buffet, looking for ideas. He would eventually bring coffee back to the room for Grace. But first he would peruse the buffet, hoping to find something interesting. Just his opinion, but breakfast is the most boring meal of the day—eggs and bread, bread and eggs—and the chef in him was scouring the morning smorgasbord for culinary inspiration. Something he could take back home with him to cook up for Grace.

"I could eat a mule," said a puffy older man, wielding tongs to load his breakfast plate. Thomas noted his silver hair, barbered with such total lack of imagination as to announce to the whole room a man without benefit of a wife.

"Not something I'd advise," replied Thomas. "This is probably the last place in America where mules are taken seriously."

"Well, it's probably as close as I'll ever get to one." The man explained that this was his sixth day at Canyon Lodge, stumbling down to the lobby at 5:30am to renew his spot on the standby list. And still nothing. "The worst part," he said, "is that damned receptionist. She's up even earlier than that, all put together and cool as a cucumber. She won't tell me where I stand on the wait list. She won't tell me how many people are on it, or if Bright Angel ever actually takes anyone from the damn standby list. All I know is if you miss a morning you're bumped, and you'll never get a mule."

"You've been waiting six days for a mule?"

"Not like I've got a lot of choice. I can't leave Arizona until I saddle up and ride down the Canyon. It's on my Bucket List."

"Your what?" said Thomas, interrupting his breakfast detective work.

"Bucket list, man. Everybody's got one. The day after I retired I made out mine, and I've been checking 'em off ever since."

"Bucket?" said Thomas.

"Yeah. Like the things you plan to do before you kick the bucket. See the Northern Lights, stand on the Great Wall of China, visit the

Pyramids, top of the Eiffel Tower. So I got Niagara Falls—check—
'Maid of the Mist'. And Hoover Dam. Next is riding a mule down
the Grand Canyon. If I could just get a damn mule."

"These are things you want to do?"

"Sure. I guess so. Doesn't everybody? Every guy I know is trying
to get through his list first."

"So it's kind of a global scavenger hunt?"

"It's a bucket list, OK? If you don't mind me asking, what's on
yours?"

Thomas thought for a moment. "Proving the existence of God."

"Like fun," said the man. "Seriously, I bet muleback down the
Canyon trail is on your list. And I bet you've got reservations for a
mule."

Thomas turned his attention to the buffet in front of him, all culinary interest forgotten. How was he to answer? Years of parochial
school made him instinctively queasy about any sort of lying. And
yet he and Grace had been sworn to secrecy. If he told the truth, this
brushcut bucketeer would move heaven and earth to follow up any
hint that Thomas might spill. So Thomas lied.

"Nope. No interest in getting saddle sores. I'm just here for the
waters."

"The waters?"

"It's a line from 'Casablanca'."

◌℧

Back at the hotel room bearing her cup of steaming hot coffee,
Thomas rapped on the door and Grace let him in.

"This trip down the Bright Angel Trail?" said Thomas, "Is it on your bucket list?"

"My what?" said Grace, coffee unfogging her brain.

"Bucket list. Things you've convinced yourself you want to do because you've never done them and you're running out of time."

Grace gave Thomas a searching look. "You've been talking to somebody."

Thomas gave a shrug.

"No. This trip is not on my bucket list. I don't have a bucket list."

"Then?" asked Thomas.

"We needed an adventure. And not just for ourselves. You remember that we talked about how much it would mean to Rafe knowing that his housebound parents were off on a grand outdoor trek like this." It was a conversation Thomas couldn't exactly remember, but Grace's certainty always meant that something of that sort must have occurred. "And, of course, you know how fond I am of horses."

"Mules," said Thomas.

"Well, yes," said Grace. "But you'll be pleased to know that I also have a theological argument for us making this trip. See, the Grand Canyon is the closest thing I can think of to God's own library. All of the time and upheaval of this world is shelved in those colored layers of stone. I wanted to do more than stand outside and look at the building. It felt necessary to go inside and at least open a book or two, turn a few pages. So I'd know something."

"Grace," crooned Thomas.

"You could choose not to say it…," said Grace.

"A bit late for that," said Thomas, "I love you. Completely."

Her kiss tasted like coffee. He'd have it no other way.

"So. Who were you talking with at the coffee urn? Did they bring their own bucket?"

"Just some recent retiree looking for a mule."

"And..."

"Grace, I realized that there's a worm in the apple. We can take the Vasari Tour all the way to Phantom Ranch and back. But we can never tell anybody about it. No photos. No social media posts. Ever. The guy at the breakfast buffet was starving for a way to get on a mule's back. If he suspected that we cut the line, he'd start asking questions."

"We can't not tell the children," said Grace.

"In this fishbowl world we'd have to swear them to secrecy. There's a lot of people with empty buckets online trolling for a loop-hole in the Park Service's quotas. To quash any rumor Bright Angel Tours would be forced to lie, probably not very convincingly. Then if people found out that Vasari exists, the Park Service would be duty-bound to shut them down. I'm not going to lose much sleep about the celebrities, but without Vasari Tours the Havasupai can't support their holdings on national park property, and they'll lose all of it. As Teddy Roosevelt said, they'd have to go."

"Once you start lying, where do you stop?"

"It's a full mile to the bottom," said Thomas Kemp.

Chapter 2

The tall man was waiting by the mules when they arrived early the next morning. There were three mules, two with saddles and one with panniers. Tied in a line to the hitching rail, they had a look of patient resignation, like they well knew what was ahead and were in no hurry to begin it. Thomas immediately felt that something wasn't right.

Once again, the colossus was dressed in beige. A beige zippered jacket and jeans to match. Thomas had never seen beige jeans before but figured that if you're that size anything you wear would have to be custom made. He was too big for anyone's britches. But that wasn't it.

"Aren't we one mule short?" said Thomas. "Looks like we're just waiting until the Vasari trail wrangler rides up on his. Or is it hers?"

"There's no wrangler," said the beige man.

"What?" said Grace sharply, "Surely they're not sending us off down those trails leaving it to the mules to know the way."

"There's only one trail. Not even an imaginative mule could get lost."

"That's not the point," she replied. "Whoever this Vasari Tours outfit is, they've got to do more than send us off with a couple of mules and—what is that—a picnic lunch?"

"You are, of course, correct," he said.

"So?" said Grace, her impatience rising like a cloud of gnats.

"I will be leading you personally. It felt like the least I could do."

Thomas felt that sink in. This enormous man was what? Graduate student, hotel concierge, trail wrangler? Whoever he was, Thomas sensed their fates were intertwined.

"Yet," said Thomas, "there remains the fact that there are only three mules."

"Surely," said the tall man, "you don't believe that they make mules to my measure. I will be making the descent on foot."

"You'll be walking?"

"I'm confident that the mounts can keep up."

Thomas eyed the dun-colored mules. He was no judge of horse-flesh, but these were no burros. They looked capable, sinewy, taller than he had imagined. He thought about a seven-footer's stride and allowed that it might well match their long equine gait.

Their trail guide introduced them to their respective mules. Grace's mule, Faustina, he described as smaller, softer-footed, and less judgmental. Thomas's was sure-footed, if a little dogmatic, and of course sturdier, given the consequences of Thomas's gourmet history. Her name was Guadalupe.

"We haven't signed anything," said Thomas. "Liability waivers? That sort of thing?"

"Owing to the fact that Vasari Corridor Tours legally does not exist, they have no legal liability. Which means there's nothing for you to waive."

"I suppose," said Thomas, trying to achieve a jocular air, "if something goes wrong, we could sue the Havasupai."

"You could," replied their enormous guide, "but they would just deny that any of their mules ever left the corral. You'll note that they don't brand their mules. For them it's a matter of respect. And it follows that, since the mules are unmarked, the survivors would have a hard time pinning any monetary damages on the Tribe. As one might expect, the Havasupai don't actually have any money. Or insurance. But they do have lawyers."

"Survivors?" mouthed Grace to Thomas. He shrugged. This vacation was, after all, her idea.

The Kemp's tour leader then explained that the principal hazard in descending the Bright Angel Trail is dehydration. It may seem paradoxical, but it gets hotter the further down into the canyon you go. Much hotter. The amount of drinking water you need in full sun at the rim is only a fraction of your hydration needs near the bottom.

Thomas was, of course, thinking of a much more abrupt form of danger. He fixed his gaze on Guadalupe's large sidelong eye, trying to gauge any possible homicidal or suicidal thoughts in there. Beneath her long lashes the mule's eye was expressionless, unreadable.

"Just to be clear," said the tall man, "the Grand Canyon is home to mountain lions, black bears, coyotes, bobcats, and foxes. Not to mention six species of rattlesnakes, the Giant Desert Hairy Scorpion and several other scorpion species, black widow spiders, tarantulas, and the Gila Monster, America's only venomous lizard."

"That was extremely clear," said Grace.

The rest of their guide's spiel, about the risks of sudden weather events and the like, sounded like something the cabin crew of an airplane tells its passengers just before takeoff. If you're a nervous person, one who has never flown before.

"Above all, trust your mule. She is more interested in getting home safe than you are."

His speech concluded, he turned to the mules. Bending in ways that would impress a giraffe, he inspected the girths and other tack, talking quietly to the animals. He helped his riders mount and adjusted their stirrups. Thomas gripped the saddle horn with both hands as if it were a control lever. He looked back at Grace who was settling into her seat like a hen on a familiar egg. They were actually going to do it. Ride mules down to the bottom of the Grand Canyon.

"One more question before we begin," said Thomas. "We're going to be together for the next two days, and we still don't know your name…"

"Robert," the tall man said with a smile.

"Do you prefer Rob or Bob?" said Grace, seeking to be polite.

"Robert is best. Robert Zimmerman," he replied, untying the pack mule from the hitching rail. As the seven-footer fidgeted with the muleback load, Thomas motioned Grace to amble her mule nearer to him, further from their guide.

"Robert Zimmerman?" Thomas whispered. "Something's not right about that. He doesn't look the least bit Jewish."

"Thomas, seriously," Grace said. "That's not worthy of you."

"Grace, do you know who Robert Zimmerman is?" said Thomas. "That's the real name of Bob Dylan."

Grace thought about it for a moment, then said, "OK. But which is more likely? A guy well over seven feet tall trying to be incognito? Or you doing your impression of Doubting Thomas?"

Was he being foolish? Probably.

"It's all part of my nightclub act," Thomas quipped back. "Theologians: North American Tour."

In five long steps Robert Zimmerman was back at the head of the mule string. And the three of them set off down the canyon. Their picnic lunch followed on behind.

The first thing they noticed about the Bright Angel Trail was the Bright Angel Trail. It unfolded before them like shiny ribbon through this corrugated landscape, appearing and vanishing in innumerable twists and switchbacks. It seemed more painted on the rock face than built into it. It showed itself in strands of trail perched along the sides of sheer cliffs. It would take an act of faith to believe that all those snippets of ribbon could somehow be contiguous. It was beautiful. And nothing about it looked safe or sane.

"How many switchbacks?" Grace elevated her voice to be heard by their trail leader.

"The number," said Robert, "isn't what matters. You'll experience each one as we get to it, and every one of them feels different." He was silent for a few more pensive paces. "You could count them on your way down. But if you count again on the return trip, I guarantee your number will be different."

Faustina ambled dutifully after their walking guide, and Thomas's long-eared Guadalupe followed behind down the absurdly narrow path. Thomas leaned back in the saddle as he had been instructed and observed Grace's sure sway. He tried not to look down, though each time the lead mule kicked a pebble over the edge he couldn't help but follow its descent.

He thought of all those well-worn phrases: The Fall of Man. To Fall from Grace.

The trail came to a massive wall of tan brown rock directly in front of them. Carved through the stone buttress was a crude rectangular passage. This was The Tunnel, the first landmark of the trail, Mile 0.1, according to their pamphlet map. Thomas had been expecting something more finished, something more like his idea of a tunnel. Then he thought: "I'm inside the Grand Canyon. The most profound example of the slow action of nature and time. And I'm fixated on a man-made hole in the rock."

Up ahead Robert entered into The Tunnel, seeming to fill the space with his extraordinary height. Cast into dark shadow, then surrounded in a nimbus of light from the far side of the opening. Then Grace on her mule went through the same transitions of light. The most natural thing in the world.

From the South Rim the canyon had been a great stone layer cake, barren rock revealed. Striations of white and brown and red and every shade between. Rock of ages. That was what Thomas was here for. Get his mind off trail and mules, or all he'd remember would be the narrowness of the track, the fear of falling, and the plodding rhythm of Guadalupe.

From the South Rim the canyon seemed barren, but here he could see it was teeming with tenacious living things. Tough woody plants grew everywhere they could find a purchase on the sheer rock. Rustles of hidden life. Little rock lizards sunning. Still as stone or scurrying for cover. Flick of Guadalupe's ear. Where you have mules, you have flies.

Thomas had read that everything changes as you descend. He silently pledged himself to not miss it. They would cross five climatic zones today before they reached the Colorado River. Each zone with its own distinct plant and animal life. Like everything else about the Grand Canyon, this vertical compression of latitude scrambles any normal sense of space and time. Trust your mule. She is more interested in getting home safe than you are.

Up ahead, their guide was walking backwards down the trail, observing them, as if hiking backwards was the easiest thing in the world. Which made Thomas nervous. What if he tripped, fell, injured himself? Thomas tried to imagine Grace and himself attempting to hoist that colossal inert broken body, somehow sling him across the back of a mule. The impossibility of turning mules around on this narrow track. Then trying to lead them back up the trail to medical aid. They were alone out here. Three people. Three mules. Anything could happen.

Up ahead, Robert was looking back at Thomas, gesturing to him. A man of normal height could hardly be seen past Faustina with Grace mounted on her back. Robert was impossible to miss.

"Whoa," said the enormous man.

Robert walked back to Thomas, passing Faustina on the abyss side, which certainly didn't seem responsible. One nervous mule kick...

He slung a half-filled plastic bag over Thomas's saddle horn.

"Stuff flies off the rim. It's unfortunate but unavoidable. We're duty-bound to pick up the trash as we go. If you don't mind being the repository." He unfolded his enormous hand to reveal a half-dozen additional pieces of litter which he stuffed into the sack on the stitched leather horn.

"I thought to take this occasion to give you some pointers on how to move with your steed." Guadalupe shook her ears at the word. Was she pleased by, or objecting to, being called a "steed"? Thomas couldn't tell. "You are moving with the mount, which is good. But you're letting her slip you around on the saddle. The end result of which will be a degree of chafing you truly don't want. She doesn't own the saddle; you do." Robert pointed at areas of improvement, tapping the saddle with a six-inch finger.

Ten feet in front, Faustina took the opportunity of a halt to plop a load of manure on the trail ahead. Lowering her long tail, she swished it with satisfaction.

"I can tell," said Robert, "that you love Grace more than the world."

Leaving Thomas, he resumed his place at the head of the mule string, and they proceeded down the Bright Angel Trail.

When you're in a line of mules navigating a tight switchback, you can have the momentary perception that you are meeting yourself, eight feet below, heading the other way. This is, of course, an illusion.

According to *A Field Guide to Geologic Time* they were now in the mid-Jurassic. At least he thought so. Thomas had brought the book in his saddlebag, hoping to check the canyon against the guidebook. But he quickly found that reading in the saddle is not possible. Besides, as their mules scraped past a cliff of stone they were within a sedimentary layer. There was no opportunity to contrast it with the ones above and below. They were too close to the subject matter.

Two switchbacks later Robert again called a halt and walked back to Thomas.

"It is fully understandable," said Robert, only a little above eye-level of the muleback-mounted theologian. "That you feel you need to lead Guadalupe through these tight turns by pulling her head with the reins. However, she is not an automobile. Your mule knows where the trail goes and wants to stay on it. Think of the reins as a reassurance, not a controller. Both of you will more greatly enjoy the ride."

Thomas nodded, feeling a bit like a schoolboy. Their guide indicated the litter bag on the saddle horn and Thomas held it open. Unfurling the fingers of his giant hand, Robert dropped in three items: an aluminum can and a mylar wrapper both featuring the word ENERGY, and a scrap of newspaper. Thomas glimpsed the headline on the paper "Grand Canyo…" and the date on the masthead: 1919.

As soon as Robert resumed his place at the head of the caravan, Thomas rummaged in the rubbish. He wasn't mistaken. The newsprint was a bit discolored and tattered, but that was no explanation. The paper was dated February 26, 1919. Well over a hundred years ago.

They moved through knife-edge contrasts of sun and shadow. Swaying gently to the steady cadence of four walking feet. Up ahead Grace was taking photos with her cell, alive to everything around her.

After a pair of horseshoe curves so tight as to seem a single broad "S" on the cliffside, the track opened up temporarily to a wide plateau. Here a mule could actually turn around. Which answered the question. In an emergency, how would you go back up the trail? By going down the trail.

"As you prefer, you can dismount here and stretch your legs or stay saddleback. Either way, drinking water is not at personal preference. It is mandatory."

Thomas slipped from the saddle. His feet hit the ground about a second before his legs buckled, landing him on his knees. His thighs had apparently taken a vacation and were reluctant to get back to work. They complained about it. But he rose and dusted himself off, rubbing a kneecap as he walked over to Grace. A horsewoman serene on her mount, surveying the far canyon walls. He handed the scrap of newspaper up to her.

"What's this?" she said.

"I don't know," said Thomas, "but it's got me spooked."

"Spooked? Please Thomas, not today."

"Just look at it, Grace."

Grace inspected the masthead of the Flagstaff Banner and the torn-off block print headline. Then she turned it over.

"It's only printed on one side."

"Look at the date, Grace. No piece of newsprint could survive a hundred years out here. Look at the condition of the paper."

"It's only printed on one side."

"So?" said Thomas.

"This isn't a newspaper. It's a replica of a newspaper. Grand Canyon National Park was founded in 1919. This is probably a facsimile made for the Centennial."

"Oh," said Thomas. "Still. It's over five years old. Pretty weird that it held up that well."

"Hydrate, Thomas, hydrate."

Chapter 3

A young man was hiking up the trail, knapsack slung, walking poles in each hand. He looked about 35 years old, habitually tanned, wearing an Aussie hat.

"Hey. I mean whoa. Nice mules. Did you know that when you get a bunch of mules together it's called a Span of Mules. Just found that out. Good to know things."

Thomas saw Grace stiffen, transfixed by this trail hiker.

"Yes," said Thomas, distracted, "thanks for the information."

"Got more, man. Just came from Havasupai Gardens. It's primo. You'll love it. Just one little glitch. The power's down. Something about a cable. Wouldn't mention it except. Like the latrines are really, really dark. Flashlight country."

"We'll just be passing through," said Thomas. "Going all the way to Phantom Ranch."

"Good on you! Hey. You folks have an awesome day. Hate to break it, but news: the way back out is 100% uphill. Didn't see that coming? Truth? Anyway, gotta get back to it. This trail won't hike itself." And with that the young man stepped past them on the safe rocky side and proceeded up the trail they just came down.

The tension in Grace was palpable. All of the tiny movements were quelled. Seated on a standing mule, Grace was as still as an equestrian statue.

"For a moment," said Grace. "That hiker. He looked…looked exactly like Rafe."

The resemblance had escaped Thomas. But mothers have a connection. Rafe was their middle child, sandwiched between two daughters. Rafe was the constant undercurrent of Grace's thoughts. He was their trouble child.

"It wasn't Rafe," said Thomas. "He didn't sound anything like Rafe."

Though it could have been Rafe. They had left Rafe caretaking their house while they were on vacation and—Thomas couldn't help thinking it—making a complete shambles of his kitchen. But Rafe could be anywhere.

For Thomas, Rafe was a problem to be solved. And the problem with Rafe was that he could be anywhere. They had rented him a furnished apartment; that had lasted four months. Their son saw no point in living in an apartment, and even less point in keeping up with the rent. Their child was off, nomadic, and Thomas was tasked with mollifying the landlord and retrieving those possessions that Rafe currently had no interest in.

It had taken a couple of years and scores of arguments, but Thomas had finally arrived at the conclusion that Rafe wasn't irresponsible. He was just differently responsible. He held down jobs. Construction mostly. He worked hard, first to arrive, last to leave. Diligent, a problem solver, generous with his help, he got along well with the crew. Until they found the burnt ends of scrap lumber in a little campfire circle, the emptied tin cans, and realized that Rafe was spending his nights on the construction site.

If it were drink or drugs, there were programs for that. But there are no rehabs for chronic lack of domesticity. Thomas paid the insurance on Rafe's pickup truck, covered the monthly bill for the cell phone he rarely answered. And prayed.

"Rafe is at our house. He's fine. We gave him a detailed chart of when to water each plant. He's not going to wander off if he's on a schedule," said Thomas. "Look, hand me your cell. I'll get a photo of his Mom on muleback, heading off down the canyon. He'll get a kick out of that." At the word 'kick' Guadalupe moved in on Faustina and gave her still-burdened sister a sympathetic nuzzle with the muzzle, bombing the snapshot.

Grace added, "We should get one with Robert."

Thomas looked around. Robert was nowhere to be seen.

But Grace was still thinking of Rafe. Not for the first time Grace started to blame herself. "We should never have sold his childhood house. The bedroom Rafe grew up in… Thomas?"

"Where's Robert?" said Thomas.

"He's probably just checking the trail up ahead."

"Did you see which way he went?" a slight note of panic in his voice. "If you were a hiker, *that* hiker, and had just passed a seven-foot man wouldn't you mention it?"

"Thomas, it's a perfect day. We're on the trip of a lifetime. OK, I brought up Rafe. But please don't get spooked about everything. No Signs and Portents. Not today."

And then Robert was over there, adjusting something on the pack mule. The mule of the unknown name. Thomas thought about it and decided not to take Robert's photo.

"Time to saddle up," said their trail guide. Thomas suddenly remembered just how rubbery his legs were. He handed the cell phone back to Grace. He rubbed the pelt of Guadalupe's coarse neck, giving himself a momentary delay. He gripped the saddle horn and braced himself to mount without assistance. Pride was involved. It wasn't elegant, but he swung into the saddle.

"Would you mind," he said to Grace, "if I rode first for a while? I have a few questions for Robert."

"The *Field Guide to Geologic Time*?"

"That," said Thomas, "and a few other things."

Grace replied, "Did you ever think what it will be like to look at the stars from the bottom of the Grand Canyon? The rocks around us will be so old and the light from the stars will have taken so long to get to us."

"The rock at the bottom of the canyon is called Vishnu Schist. It's nearly two billion years old. That's much further back in time than the light from any star that you could see."

"Older than starlight. That's heady stuff, dear."

Thomas gave Guadalupe a suggestion, which she considered. Then she followed on behind the seven-foot man.

"Sir," said Thomas, "what are the Havasupai Gardens?"

"Is," said their colossal walking guide. "Your question is what is Havasupai Gardens. It's the only campground along the trail. Halfway to Phantom Ranch. There's a stream there and it's much greener than what you see around you. Potable water, latrines, picnic tables.

It's very nice. The Havasupai tribe used to farm there, but they were relocated years and years ago. We should be there in about an hour."

"So that's how much time we've got together?"

"I don't quite grasp you meaning, Thomas."

"I called you 'Sir' as a term of respect. And because I don't believe your name is Robert Zimmerman. Or Bob Dylan, for that matter. And I don't believe that Vasari Tours exists either."

"They weren't wrong about you. You do indeed question every proposition."

"What tipped me off was the hiker. Imagine I was a famous movie star, a well-known face. And I wanted to take a mule down the Grand Canyon in secrecy. By timing it right, Vasari Tours could avoid being seen by the other, legitimate, muleback tour. But it couldn't avoid the trail hikers. And this trail heads right down through a campground full of them."

"Fifteen campsites, to be exact," said their guide.

"And even though that hotel receptionist made it abundantly clear that I wasn't a celebrity, or even a semi-famous writer, I'm still trying to imagine the effect that three unauthorized mules and a walking wrangler well over seven feet tall would have on all those campers."

"And your conclusion?"

"That whatever you brought us out here for will happen before we reach Havasupai Gardens."

"Time will take its time. And what will be, will be," said the trail guide.

So Thomas asked the big question. "In the lecture hall you said 'I miss faith' and it felt like an accusation. Is that what this is about?"

"Faith." Robert considered the word. "Yes. It acknowledges something. Something beyond what we can encompass. Where humanity is not the measuring stick. Eternal. Like the Grand Canyon."

They rode on in silence for a while. Guadalupe's hoof dislodged a pebble. Thomas heard it fall into the abyss.

"Sir, I understand that there was another canyon. Glen Canyon. In many ways it was as magnificent as the Grand Canyon. It was just upriver on the Colorado. It's gone."

"Gone?" said the giant.

"Clearly you're not as well-informed as you claim. Human free will. Specifically, the free will of the ironically-named U.S. Bureau of Reclamation. They built the Glen Canyon Dam and inundated that canyon under 25 million acre-feet of water. Blocking the Colorado River and creating Lake Powell, again ironically named. Named after John Wesley Powell, the explorer who with nine men and four fragile boats first braved the wild Colorado River and described the beauty of that canyon. One wonders how he would feel about having the artificial lake that destroyed it named after him."

"These are just the accidents of history. Of no consequence," declared their guide, though it didn't sound very convincing.

"But wait," said Thomas, "there's more. The Marble Canyon Dam just above Grand Canyon National Park and the Bridge Canyon Dam just below it. Together these would have reduced the flow of the Colorado to a 'recreational trickle' through the Grand Canyon. Effectively stopping the process of time."

"Would have?"

Thomas answered, "Owing to the economics of the moment, those two proposed hydroelectric dams were never built."

"Humanity doesn't seem to be very good at playing God," said the colossus. "Though extremely good at saying 'it seemed like a good idea at the time'."

Their guide stopped in the middle of the trail and turned to Thomas. He seemed to have something on his mind, something unsaid. Guadalupe came to a halt. Aways up the trail, Faustina too ceased her plodding gait, leaving Grace well out of earshot. Grace took the opportunity of this pause to take photos from the saddle, wholly involved in finding frames for the vastness around her.

Then the seven-foot man said quietly to Thomas: "A moment from now, your son Rafe will set down a box of oatmeal. He is unfamiliar with your professional kitchen gas range. On the lowest simmer setting the flame cycles on and off, rather than burning continuously. After he heated a kettle for tea, he thought he turned it off; instead he turned it to simmer. He's not aware of this when he sets that round box of Quaker Oats on that burner. Now he's gone to water the plants according to your strict schedule. The box of dry oatmeal forms a column of fire, sending embers throughout the kitchen. The fire spreads. When the smoke alarm goes off, he rushes back to the kitchen. Rather than getting out and calling for help, he attempts to fight the fire himself. He is not successful."

"You can't possibly know this."

"I *don't* know this," said the guide. "It hasn't happened yet. Not up there on the canyon rim. But time is a little different here."

"This is some trick, some kind of stage mentalist act. I don't know when Grace talked to you about Rafe, but you must have pumped her for details."

"I assure you that nothing of the kind occurred. Furthermore, Grace doesn't know that in your haste to depart you failed to explain the operation of your prized five-burner chef range. That only you know."

"Why are you telling me this?" a note of panic entering his voice.

"Because there is time," said the guide.

"Time?" said Thomas, feeling bewildered. "You said it hasn't happened yet. If it hasn't happened, then is it still possible for it not to happen?"

"That's in your hands, Thomas."

Thomas took the full weight of it in. His voice was hoarse with emotion as he whispered, "This would break Grace utterly. That her son died in a fire that destroyed our home. While she was on vacation."

The beige-clad man grasped Guadalupe's bridle and they started walking together. The other mules ambled on behind. "They were right about you," he said softly. "When faced with calamity, you don't think about yourself first. Thomas Kemp, a good and blameless man, you don't rush to bewail your fate, to cry like Job how unfair God is being to you *personally*. Your heart rushes to safeguard Grace."

"Grace *is* my heart. I love her as wife and companion, best friend, counterpoint and contradictor. One flesh, we treasure, complete, and correct each other. But beyond that, I love her mother's heart. She would suffer anything for her children, especially Rafe, who flounders. She gave them life. And giving birth is a lifelong process. I see it every single day but it remains a mystery.

"Have mercy on her. On us. She will take the blame on herself. She loaned Rafe our home, insisted he stay while we traveled. Hoping our vacation would somehow change him. Cure his wandering. It just can't end this way. With Grace texting canyon photos home, each composed as a gift, to a charred and silent ruin."

The impossibly tall man walked on in silence, seemingly considering Thomas' declaration. Then he spoke. "The management regrets to inform you that The Beatles were wrong. Love is not all you need."

"It's my Proof, isn't it?" said Thomas, "You've come to punish me for my hubris. The erosion of faith. Making God no more than a comforting inevitability, a logical conclusion. Proving His existence with cosmology, particle physics, and duct tape."

"It's a pretty big ask," said Robert.

"Listen, I don't know whether I'm talking to an angel, a lunatic, or just a storyteller with a grudge. And, Sir, it doesn't matter. Because we are alone here in the womb of time. Surrounded by the fossilized bones of all life that has ever been on earth. As our guide you have the responsibility to protect. Or the ability to lead us into calamities."

"My only charge is to walk you down the Bright Angel Trail. Deliver you to Phantom Ranch," said the mule wrangler.

"Stop, for mercy's sake. This is Rafe. My only son. I am here, in this rift in the earth, pleading with you for his life. You said there is still time. If it is within whatever power you have, preserve the Kemps from what is to come." Thomas took a deep breath. "For that I am willing to renounce my Proof, to recant all that I have done trying to turn faith into knowledge," said Thomas. "I was wrong, Sir.

Now I see my fatal flaw. Annihilation does not leave Nothing. Faith remains. Belief in things unseen. It's the thing we need most."

The messenger released the mule's bridle. He nodded to Thomas. He then said, "Those are words, Thomas. You are good with words."

Then Robert raised his voice loud enough for Grace on the second mule to hear. "Up ahead on your right you'll see a fault line. That's where one layer of geological time is thrust up to cross over the newer layers. You can see the different colors. Huge tectonic forces were involved. To all appearances this is a place where time is confused."

"Genesis 32:24," said Thomas quietly.

"Sorry," said Robert, "Not familiar."

"Jacob wrestled with an angel. And Jacob said, 'I will not let thee go, except thou bless me.'"

Their seven-foot-tall guide turned his back and continued hiking down the Bright Angel Trail.

Thomas fumbled with his saddlebag. Unhooking the buckle, he pulled out *A Field Guide to Geologic Time*. He threw the paperback book down on the trail. Guadalupe flinched at the unexpected sound; her withers bristled beneath his hand. Stomped her hoof in protest. Their guide heard the book fall and stopped in his tracks.

Behind him he could feel Grace stiffen, alert, ready to intervene on his behalf. Feisty Grace, defender in battle. But she didn't know, couldn't know, why Thomas had thrown down this challenge. He waved her off. Then he locked his gaze with the leader of mules.

"I don't know what you're trying to prove," said Robert, "but this is hardly worthy of you. Kindly dismount and pick your book up off the trail."

"No," said Thomas.

"No?"

"Nope. I'm through with it. It's just words."

"You're just going to leave it there?" said their trail guide.

"A clover, a speck of lint. Or, should I say, a piece of litter."

"Is this how thou would wrestle with me? By littering?"

"Sir," said Thomas, "I have on the horn of my saddle a sack of rubbish. All of the human-made trash that you collected from the Bright Angel Trail. Wrappers made of polyethylene terephthalate, plastics that will endure for thousands of years. Should I choose to," he glanced over the edge of the narrow trail to the abyss below, "I could release all that to the winds. Past anyone's ability to retrieve. Tarnishing the Bright Angel Trail for generations."

"This is absurd. You wouldn't do that."

"It's not the size of the act," said Thomas. "It's the choice that we make to act. Human free will. For well or for ill. The choice to act. No matter how small. To spit in the eye of fate. To scatter everything you gathered." Thomas unhooked the litter bag from his saddle horn.

Robert's gaze was steady, unfathomable. "Thomas, you indeed have free will. And actions are louder and deeper than words. But malevolence isn't freedom. It's a prison. You don't need me to tell you that."

"It's the only leverage I have." His voice came out like a whimper.

"I am just a guide down the trail," said Robert. "A messenger. I have no power to change the trail itself. But eons of history are exposed in this canyon. We see time more clearly. There are switchbacks. Things that are yet to be can be seen before they arrive. Or not arrive. Accidents may be averted."

Thomas paused, looked back at Grace, then looped the trash bag handles back on his saddle horn. "If we are not led to temptation, then we can be delivered. To give up whatever puny power we have as an act of faith. That's what Jacob wrestled with. A litterbug on the Bright Angel Trail. A fire in a kitchen."

Guadalupe kicked a pebble over the edge. Startled, a scrub jay flew across the trail.

Robert held up both his hands. Grace saw it as a signal to halt. She neatly dismounted Faustina and stood by her mount, working the cramps out of her legs. Thomas saw it as a gesture of surrender.

"On the occasion of your arrival at Havasupai Gardens," their guide said to Thomas, "your mules will seamlessly rejoin their equine tribe as if they had never been parted. The Bright Angel Tour wranglers will welcome you as the last arrivals in their tour group. They will ask what took you so long. My best advice would be to blame the mules."

Robert lowered his hands. He bent down to pick up the guidebook from the trail and handed it back. Before he turned away, he said quietly, "Thomas, I bless you. Go in peace."

"Thank you," said Thomas to the empty canyon air.

Grace walked up to where Thomas sat mounted on Guadalupe. She looked around. "Where's Robert? And what was *that* all about?"

Thomas dismounted. Locking his knees, he landed on his feet without stumbling.

"Oh," said Thomas. "Up ahead. Let's lead our mules for a while. The trail's wider, easier, here. There's no way to get lost. And there's a story I'd like to tell you along the way."

Frogs

She stood before the second graders as the children searched for their seats in this new classroom, a colorful construction paper name plate identifying each desk. She had tried to use only first names, but a few names in the roster repeated, seemingly again and again. She had considered using pink construction paper for girls and blue for boys, but there were too many names that could have been either. She wondered, not for the first time, whether modern parents select just one name and apply it equally to boy or girl. Or do they still pick two baby names, then live forever with the phantom, named but never existing? The girl they didn't have when they did have a boy.

Once the children were all settled, Danielle Milner commenced. She pointed to an aquarium on her desk, its greenish pond water astir with faint wriggles of life.

"If there is one thing that you will learn in this classroom, it's that tadpoles turn into frogs."

She then called the children one by one to the front of the class to look in the murky glass tank and make their reports.

"It's a bunch of black fish."

"The proper term is 'school.' And no, they're not fish. Tadpoles are amphibians."

"These *amphibians*," said the next student, "are all hiding under the grassy stuff in there."

"They probably saw your shadow when you leaned over the tank," said their teacher, Mrs. Milner, "They're afraid that you're going to eat them." This was greeted by a collective "Eeew."

"They're *ugly*," said the third student who came forward, obviously pleased to be able to say that out loud.

"We'll come back to that judgment later. After we've gotten to know them."

"How can we *know* them? They're, like, *fish*."

"If they were fish, they would just become bigger fish. But these are tadpoles, and we're going to watch them turn into frogs."

"Won't that take a really, *really* long time?"

"Yes. But while we're waiting, we're going to observe everything about them. Especially how they talk to each other."

The children eyed the dull blunt creatures as they swam slowly from one bit of edible green to another. No one held their breath waiting for them to talk.

ભ

"How did it go babe? First day in the classroom and all?" said Simon.

"I think it went well," said Danielle. "Hard to say. I brought in the tadpoles, and we watched them swimming around. I don't think anyone believes in frogs yet."

"That's what I love about you, wife. You believe in frogs."

"It helps to have a prince to kiss," Danielle said, moving in closer.

But her husband's mind was still on pollywogs. "So what's next with the experiment?"

"Tomorrow," she said, "we give each child their own tadpole."

"But they all look the same."

"I know. And they're all named Alex or Aiden, Logan or Dakota."

"You know what I mean…"

"That's why I got these ink markers from the biology supply house. Non-toxic to amphibia but permanent. And wonderfully colorful. No more drab little pollywogs."

"Are you sure that's a good idea?"

"Your point being…"

"Unless I've very mistaken, not all of your baby frogs are going to make it. Do you really want to explain to a student that their own personal pollywog is floating belly up?"

Danielle thought about it. You wanted each child to have a positive educational experience. But positive wasn't the same thing as guaranteed safe. She could hope for a semester without incident. And she could cope with so minor and instructive a calamity as that, should it occur.

ೞ

"Mrs. Milner," said Olivia whose hand shot up like a signal flag. "There are *two* fishbowls on your desk today."

"*Amphibian* bowls," corrected the girl behind her.

"You are absolutely right. They're called tanks, or aquaria."

"*Amphibian aquaria,*" repeated the little girl, dazzled by the sound of it all.

"The tadpoles in this big tank that I brought in yesterday all came from the same gelatinous floating mass of translucent eggs." Someone in the back was able to visualize this enough to say "*Eeew*," and the rest of the classroom took up the chorus. "What that means is that all these tadpoles are brothers and sisters. And I thought that you wouldn't want to be stuck in a school with just your sisters and brothers. So I brought another family of baby frogs in this little fish tank. I'm going to put a little colored mark on the back of each of their heads so we can tell the families apart, then we're going to mix them up in the big tank and let them all be in class together."

The children watched Mrs. Milner use a little net to catch each tadpole in turn, then dab the back of its head with a tiny red dot. Some of the children really wanted to "paint" the pollywogs, but she had to disappoint them. Marking dye is extremely permanent. She'd seen what second graders could do with poster paint. Sending children home with indelible stains on their fingers? Not a good idea.

A red dot for one batch of future froglets, a blue dot for the other. And voila! Pouring a wriggling stream from the small glass box to the big aquarium she declared them the Montagues and the Capulets. Poured pond water smelled nothing like roses, but what's in a name?

"Mounty-glue?"

"Caplet!"

The class clustered around all four sides of the glass tank. Would the Montague brothers and sisters stick together when put in with strangers, or would they make new friends? There were as many opinions as pollywogs so they talked about ways to find out who was right. Lots of good questions from these budding scientists.

As she drove home she reflected on it. A really productive class-room experience.

That evening her husband said, "You haven't handed out indi-vidual tadpoles yet?"

"First we will study group dynamics, then we'll chart the emer-gence of personality."

"Sounds highly academic when you say it that way, babe," he said with that growly purr in his voice. "You know," he said, "you can't put it off indefinitely. They're going to want to give them names. So can we at least talk about names? I'm getting pretty tired of 'Baby Bump'. I know. It's too soon. Still, could we maybe not have some second grader give a frog the same name we're giving our son. Our child. Child. Daughter is fine, perfect in fact if that's what Baby Bump wants to be. Ten fingers, ten toes, that's all that matters. And a name that doesn't sound like a frog."

The next morning a Capulet was found floating on the algae sur-face. Dead. Danielle netted it up and threw it in the trash can under her desk before the students arrived.

Before they took their seats the children clustered around the tank on the front desk. Danielle hoped that no one was counting tadpoles.

"They're *kissing*," said a girl named Amelia.

"Probably not. They're just both trying to eat the same little bite of breakfast."

"Kissing," said Amelia.

"So," said Mrs. Milner, "here's the science question for the day. Come up to the aquarium one by one. When you see two tadpoles touch each other I want you to make a mark on the whiteboard and then go back to your seat. Then the next student will come up and do the same thing. If both tadpoles are from the same family, make a mark here. If they are from different families make a mark over there.

After one session of amphibian observation, the children took their seats and were led through arithmetic and spelling. When they needed a little break, she held another round of Tadpoles Touching. And the marks started adding up on the whiteboard.

൬

In the evening they shared the dining table they never used for dining in convivial silence. Simon hunched over his multi-tester, watching the meter flicker as he probed some electronic gizmo spidery with wires. Danielle shuffled through the children's spelling papers. She was struggling to find a way to teach spelling, something beyond right and wrong. Writing words by sound was only taking them so far. There had to be some way to get them to both hear the word in their heads and see the letters lined up at the same time.

"I've been thinking about names all day," Simon said. "I think for a girl it should be 'Polly'. If it's a boy, 'Tad'."

"Interesting choices."

"Seriously, how do you tell boy tadpoles from girl tadpoles?"

"You can't."

"I know I can't," said Simon. "And maybe you can't either. But surely some kind of frog expert can tell the pollys from the tads."

"That's where it gets messy. There really aren't boy tadpoles and girl tadpoles. If you want to sacrifice one and thin slice the corpse, and you happen to have an electron microscope handy, you can determine what sex it was. At that time."

"You didn't just say that, did you?"

Danielle continued, "Like a lot of creatures, frogs don't have sex chromosomes. Who they turn out to be has a lot to do with environmental factors."

"OK…" he said, "How about the ones croaking in the pond?"

"Oh those are definitely males. Loud and proud with the vocal sacs to prove it. But unless they're singing it's still pretty hard to tell. Naturally, they don't have a penis."

"Ummm, I'm not sure I like where this is going. So what do they have?"

"Back when public schools thought frog dissection was educational, they had us looking through the viscera for internal testes," said Danielle. "Frog balls."

"Let's stick with the live ones on the lily pads."

"Pads is exactly right. The guys have nuptial pads. Calluses on their hands that help them get a grip on that slippery female."

"Every day I imagine I couldn't love you more. And every day you confound expectation," he said, placing his nuptial pads around her barely visible swelling. "But promise me something," he murmured.

"Anything."

"That you won't repeat a word of what you just explained to me within five miles of a public school."

❧

Tadpoles Touching had been good observational science, but the same-family count and the different-family count were almost the same. The children had expected some dramatic result and were disappointed.

"Maybe," said Lucius, "there's just one tadpole who goes around bumping into all the other ones."

"Yeh," said another boy. "They all look the same."

"And they're *still* ugly," said a third.

Mrs. Milner pointed at the tallies on the whiteboard. "Every experiment asks a question and gives an answer. The answer we got this time was Nothing. I know that was not the result that any of you were hoping for. But often the best answers are the ones that are a surprise. What we found out in Tadpole Touching was whether the tadpoles are brothers and sisters doesn't matter. And that negative answer asks more and better questions. Maybe tadpoles can't tell who they are related to. Or don't care. Or maybe Lucius is right. Maybe not all tadpoles behave the same." The point was made, and their interest rekindled for a moment. But without dramatic results her student's attention was starting to drift. Time to move on.

"We want to name the tadpoles," said Olivia.

"The tadpoles need names." Several children spoke up in agreement.

Mrs. Milner held up her hand in surrender. "Yes. But if we're going to name them we have to be able to tell them apart. So here's our next question. If we have thirty tadpoles and half are marked blue and half are marked red, how many more color dots will they need for every one to be different?"

"You mean if one has blue and blue?"

"And blue and red? And red and red. That's only three."

"We have yellow dye and white dye too," added Mrs. Milner helpfully.

"Seven?" said Liam, who didn't sound very sure about it.

She moved to the whiteboard and started drawing lines across and then lines down. She assigned each row and column a color name. A grid of possibilities.

The children looked lost for a minute, then Liam smiled and said "Eight."

"Why eight, not seven?"

"Because there's blue and red and there's red and blue. They're different names."

"And if we had three color dots?" She could almost hear the mental gears spinning.

The other kids pushed Liam forward. Right or wrong he would speak for all of them. "Three dots. One is red or blue. The other two can be any color." She held out the whiteboard marker, but Liam ignored it, lost in mental mathematics. "Four times four times two." Liam paused, his eyes on the ceiling. "Thirty-two. Thirty-two names. Three dots are enough names for all thirty tadpoles."

Twenty-nine tadpoles, thought Danielle Milner.

Enough math for one day. It was time for recess. The kids leapt to the playground field like running was water. Good, get out the wiggles, thought Mrs. Milner. They would charge around for every last second before being reeled in. Except one. She came back to the classroom before the others, clutching a ragged little bouquet of buttercups. Sweet. Danielle offered to surrender her coffee cup as a vase.

"No. They're for the tadpoles."

"Olivia, that's lovely, but I don't think pollywogs eat buttercups."

"Not to eat. I want the flowers to float on the top. Then when they look up they'll see flowers. They'll know that heaven is pretty. And they won't be sad."

"Sad?" said Mrs. Milner.

"Cause one of their sisters went to heaven."

She was about to ask if Olivia had somehow counted the twenty-nine constantly criss-crossing tadpoles. Then she realized it had nothing to do with counting.

"Are you sad?" said Danielle.

Olivia didn't answer. She just held her fistful of buttercups. "They're my *friends*," said Olivia.

When the rest of the class returned, flushed with victories, Danielle handed out a calm-down assignment, geography worksheets: read the map and answer questions. This town is in which state, which states border the ocean, which ones are divided by this river. Most adults could do it in a few minutes. She knew it would take her class much longer than that. While they were occupied, she opened the locked supply cabinet and brought out the marking dyes. One by one she netted the pollywogs and uniquely identified them.

She was about halfway through when it happened. There was a fuzziness on the edges of her vision. She started blinking, but that only made the fuzziness seethe. Then Nothing. There was no experience of it happening, no sense of duration, no memory that it had happened. Just a jump forward in time. The blue permanent marking dye was spilled across her desktop and a drop of it was staining the back of her hand.

The children were all suddenly as alert as prairie dogs. When consciousness returned as if it had never disappeared, Danielle Milner said, "Everything is all right, children."

But it wasn't.

She asked Miss Praeger to take over her class until the lunch break. Praeger is an alarmist who was three finger pokes away from dialing 911, but Danielle dissuaded the ambulance call. "I'm just a little overtired. I'll go rest for a bit in the break room."

Well. If there weren't rumors about the pregnancy already, there surely were now.

In the break room she nursed a tall black coffee, though she knew that would do nothing to help the situation. Her fellow teacher Pam Gillett came in, closed the door behind her, and gave her the eye. "So. You look like you've seen a ghost."

"A ghost of my own childhood. I had these for over a year, undiagnosed, when I was in grade school. My third-grade teacher thought I was just a dreamy kid. Off in a world of my own. She called it 'unicorns and butterflies'.

"But it's not imagined unicorns or clouds forming shapes in the sky. It's not anything. It's just a lapse, a blank space. My parents thought I wasn't getting enough sleep. They restricted my TV watching time, sent me to bed early. But it turned out those little 'naps' were happening forty or fifty times a day. And it didn't matter what I was doing: sitting, standing, even running. I was playing freeze tag with myself.

"When the breakfast spoon halts halfway to your mouth and nothing that anyone says gets through, that's not a daydream. It's ten seconds out of your life of which you have no memory. It's like everything stops to reboot."

"We grew up in the Good Old Days, when everything was a *character* issue," said Pam Gillett.

"They say it affects psychosocial development. I think what that means is that *nobody* wants to be your friend.

"It was my fourth-grade teacher who finally put a name to it, and the name was a kind of French poetry: *petit mal,* the little illness. I believe that I'm a teacher because of her. She was smart enough to see it, and compassionate enough to convince my parents to see it too.

"My parents didn't want to believe that their perfect little daughter had a seizure disorder. Doesn't that mean you collapse and writhe around on the floor biting your own tongue? That's the operatic version, the *grand mal.* I was the musical comedy version, forgetting my lines and staring off into space.

"It took a doctor and an EEG to finally call it by its proper name: absence seizures. It's something that develops in childhood and gets outgrown in adolescence. Except not always. In my case, not always. There's medication that controls it. But."

"But," said Pam Gillett, "you can't take the meds if you're pregnant. Or trying to be."

଄

She told her husband when he got home from the job site.

"And you *drove* home?"

"What else was I supposed to do? My car was in the school parking lot. I felt fine. And I'd only had the one."

"That you know of. From everything you've told me you have no memory of your lapses. You just check out. Then check back in again. Probably you have no idea how many you've had. What if you're behind the wheel the next time it happens?"

"But I wasn't."

Simon threw up his hands, walked to the other side of the kitchen. With his back to her he said to no one in particular: "When you came off your meds you knew this was possible. Likely."

She walked over to him and put her arms around him from behind, holding him to her.

"It's what we chose for the health of our baby. We both know that if I was on those medications our baby..." she said. "And our baby is safe, thank God. That's what matters." She stood on tiptoes to nuzzle her belly into the small of his back. "Fortunately, I had the presence of mind to waive off the call for the EMTs. Had the ambulance guys shot me up with their drugs who knows what would have happened."

He turned to face her. "You weren't the only one making a choice. I had to choose to send you off day after day with a smile, knowing that sooner or later you'd space out."

"It was just one little absence. Couldn't have been longer than ten seconds."

Simon pointed to the indelible blue mark on her hand. "In front of a whole classroom of students. While handling permanent dye."

"Small price..."

"Yes, but you're not the only one paying it. Whether you've noticed or not, I've been paying it too. Every day on the job site, checking my cell phone, hoping the call will be from you and not someone else. And now those children. It didn't go unnoticed. You scared them. They probably thought you'd died and were waiting for you to fall over. In fact, you have no idea what went on with them. Because you simply weren't there."

"You're right. I should have prepared them. Explained it to them."

"And then how about explaining to their parents that at any random moment their child will be wholly unsupervised, their teacher absent in some fog? You can't continue."

"But I have to. The kids. And the tadpoles."

"Someone else, maybe that Miss Praeger, can take over the tadpoles."

"Miss Praeger would *not* be good with pollywogs. Besides, this is my project. I've got to see it through."

"A three-month classroom project that you created *after* you stopped taking the Valproate. Like you were daring the fates to try and stop you."

"You knew I was a teacher when you married me."

Simon put his arms around her and held on tight. But she could hear him thinking.

"Yeah," he said. "I guess I had no idea what that meant."

They made dinner together and she watched him watch her. Every time she held a knife or put something on a burner. He was a man and he loved her. He would protect her, whether she wanted him to or not.

Pregnancy had done odd things to her appetite. Meals used to make sense, you knew when you would be hungry and how much would fill you up. Now there was no telling. As the smell of cooking filled the kitchen her appetite retreated. She knew it would be back, wolfish, probably when she should be sleeping. She sat before her plate and watched her husband eat.

"You're right," she said. "Driving to school is just too dangerous. I'm going to stop."

Simon put down his fork. He was preparing a response, probably some mix of praise for being sensible combined with a heartfelt wish that things were otherwise and that she could continue in the classroom doing what she loves. She spared him the effort.

"No more driving. I'm going to take the school bus."

"The bus? You mean the yellow bus with the fourth and fifth graders? That bus?"

"Why not?"

"It's got to be against some kind of regulation."

"I'd like to see them try to enforce it."

 ❦

"Teacher moved lots of tadpoles," announced a small child to no one in particular.

Yes, she had. The families were still mixed together, but only half of the tadpoles were still in the big aquarium. Danielle had shifted the other half to the small fish tank. She made sure there was plenty of food in both. Then she asked the students why.

"The ones in the big tank have more room."

"Yeah, but now my fish is in the little tank, and he's all crowded."

"*Amphibian*," corrected another student.

"Students, if these tanks were real frog ponds, one would be a big pond and one would be a little pond. What could happen to a little pond that wouldn't happen to a big pond?"

"It could all dry up."

"That's right. They're called vernal pools. And what would happen to the tadpoles in that little pond?"

"They'd all be *dead*!" said one boy dramatically.

"Unless what?"

One boy's hand shot up and waved around. "Unless…" he said, then he suddenly lost his confidence. "Um. They're tadpoles," he began, "Tadpoles swim." Mrs. Milner wanted desperately to cue him. But she knew enough to smile encouragingly and wait. After a glacial silence Aiden continued, "Frogs don't swim. They do. But they don't have to. They can jump." Then the idea came to him, relief visibly washing over the boy. "If the tadpoles were frogs, then they could jump out of the little pond and find the big pond."

"So the tadpoles in the little pond better hurry up and become frogs," said Mrs. Milner. "Do you think they will? Everyone can help watch."

ॐ

"Seriously. You've got to stop teaching," said Simon.

"It's just getting interesting."

"Denial isn't just a river in Egypt. Even if you're not driving, you're putting yourself at risk. And that means you're putting our baby at risk."

"Baby Bump is just fine. Bump is getting everything he needs. And the doctor said I should keep active."

"Active doesn't mean being in charge of a classroom of children. Anything could happen."

"Learning, discovery, original thinking, self-confidence," said Danielle. "Pretty much anything."

ଊଓ

Some of the pollywogs in the small tank looked odd Monday morning. It was as if they had eaten something bulky that was poking out of their sides.

"What's *wrong* with them?" said the curly-haired Sophia.

"Everything is right with them," said Mrs. Milner. "Those are the back legs."

"You mean they have legs *inside* them?" said the girl, fairly horrified at the idea.

Mrs. Milner tried to explain how these bumps were leg buds that would change into fully functioning jumping legs. Halfway through her explanation she realized she had no idea how the limb buds become attached to the tadpole skeleton. Do leg bones grow out from new-formed pollywog hips? Or do the limb buds send bony runners back deep into the living flesh to hook up with the skeleton? Either way sounded actually kind of horrifying.

Then it happened, a startle of joy. She felt the first kick.

ဘ

"Before we begin, you need to let me know what you don't want to know."

Danielle and Simon stared blankly at the sonogram technician, a stranger to them both.

"Oh yeah, that," said Simon. "We don't…" he glanced over at his wife for confirmation, her belly glossy with the warmed conductive gel. Danielle nodded. "We'd prefer to keep it a surprise. At least for now."

"That's fine. Many couples do. At this stage it's unlikely we'd know anything anyway." The carrot-haired technician applied her sensor to Danielle's swelling belly. Danielle watched the girl's hand move slowly across her bare stretched skin, the glint of an engagement ring. In this weirdly intimate moment, she felt a rush of attachment towards this young woman just starting out on the course that Danielle was on. They were whispering wordless secrets that even her beloved Simon would never be party to.

"Just one thing," said the technician. "Please don't. Don't phone the office at odd hours and leave messages. Because you're decorating the nursery, or some aunt wants to know." She moved the probe slightly lower and picked up the heartbeat. It filled every corner of the room, sloshy, fast and insistent. "We really can't," she said, "talk about sex over the telephone."

ೞ

Pam Gillett waited until Miss Praeger left the Break Room. "Danielle," she said, "We have to talk about accommodation."

"I don't need accommodation. I'm pregnant. Last I heard that wasn't classified by the ADA as a disability."

"I didn't say you *need* accommodation. What I'm saying is you need to *request* it."

Danielle took a long sip of coffee.

"Suppose," continued Pam Gillett, "you have another one of your vanishing acts in the classroom. And some parent got wind of it. You'd be on much safer ground if you could show you'd requested accommodation."

Danielle thought about it, then replied. "There's a problem with that. The law says we're entitled to accommodation if that enables us to teach despite a disability or injury. But I've been teaching here for three years without disclosing that I have a condition that necessitates accommodation for student safety. And suddenly I'm declaring it."

"It got worse," said Pam Gillett.

"No, what gets worse is my rationale for accommodation. I'm requesting it because the absence seizures are no longer controlled. And the reason they're not controlled is that I deliberately chose not to take the medication that would control them."

"Nobody needs to know all that."

"Either I've been endangering students for the past three years, or I've just now chosen to endanger students. Doesn't look so good, Pam."

"Just file the paper. By the time they get around to finding you a teaching assistant, you'll be out on maternity. By the way, how's it going with the baby?"

"Perfect. Haven't upchucked in the classroom and mostly kept quiet about my overwhelming cravings for bologna and pickles in the lunchroom."

"Is it a boy or a girl?"

"Yes."

ଓ

She wasn't in the classroom when the next lapse happened. The timing was probably the best possible. She was sitting on the morning school bus, her presence a minatory buffer between the driver and the Fifth Grade. One moment they were leaving the edge of her suburban neighborhood and the next they were pulling into the elementary school's long circular driveway. Everything in between was simply gone. No experience of it, no recollection. An absence.

Only, she realized with horror, there was one yellow house. Just glimpsed for a second. A yellow house set off by itself on a wooded lot. It wasn't in her neighborhood. It wasn't anywhere near the school. Somewhere in between. It wasn't an absence seizure. It was two. Two absences strung so close together that she had regained consciousness for just an eyeblink.

If two episodes could happen without a recovery interval, there was nothing to prevent a cascade of little seizures, like tadpoles pouring from a tank, each one nipping at the tail of the one preceding it.

Simon was right. She had put herself way out on the edge. For the gratification of seeing ideas and insights blossoming in the faces of children. For a tank of tadpoles. Who was it serving now? Not the children. They were innocent bystanders in her private war with a childhood nemesis that had taken too many moments of her life. And left holes.

The bell rang. Too late. Danielle hurried to her classroom, her head going in a thousand directions. As she passed Mrs. Gillett's room, she made a gesture meaning "keep an eye on me." Pam Gillett nodded.

In the classroom she set the students to the task of finding tadpoles with hind legs. Those on the left side of the class pressing their noses against the big aquarium, those on the right squinting through the murk into the little tank. Blue-yellow-red. Red-red-white. Lists of leggy pollywogs started accumulating on either side of the whiteboard.

Danielle took out her cell phone and positioned it in front of her on the teacher's desk, leaning it against the back of the big aquarium. She stared at the Clock app. As she led the children deeper and deeper into metamorphosis, she kept one eye on each minute as it elapsed. Counting them off. One to sixty.

Why sixty seconds in a minute? Why not some other number? Indeed, why divide up a day into hours, minutes, seconds? Assumptions worth exploring in the classroom. A new curriculum started forming in the air. Once sparked, children would have such good questions.

She kept counting off the minutes. And none of them showed up missing.

Class ended and the kids filed out to the lunchroom. Danielle exhaled. It was time to phone Simon. There was no putting it off any longer.

"Babe? Can you leave work early, swing by the school and pick me up? If it's convenient. No big deal."

"What's wrong?" he said. Danielle paused, not knowing where to begin. Simon continued in a high, pinched voice, his words tripping over each other. "Yes. Of course. Absolutely. Just. Just stay there. OK, I'm leaving now. Right now. There's something wrong."

"Nope. Your Babe and our baby are both just fine. No rush. I really…"

"What do you mean 'fine'? What's that supposed to mean? What's going on? I swear if you reassure me one more time, I'm running every red light between here and there."

Keep it breezy, Danielle.

"If you're going to insist on driving recklessly, I can take the school bus. It's only that… I just need your renowned masculine upper body strength. Aquariums are heavy."

"Aquariums?"

"Full of tadpoles. Soon to be froglets."

Silence on the line.

"You're bringing the frogs home?"

Light. "Is that a problem? I was just thinking that twenty-nine metamorphic amphibians might be just the thing we need around the house. You know, a kind of decorative accent?"

"You're bringing frogs home," said Simon.

"No, they'll be coming home as pollywogs. They're not properly called froglets until they have front legs. And they won't be jumping out of the tanks for at least another two weeks."

"I'll be right there. Don't go anywhere. Unless you have to go somewhere."

There wasn't much traffic. And laws were broken. Simon was at the door of her classroom while her children were still at lunch. Pam Gillett had offered to monitor both grades and had a combined class Enrichment up her sleeve for the afternoon, should Danielle need to leave early.

Simon paused in the doorway in his coveralls like he'd braved a tornado. He looked as if he expected to find a classroom full of first responders. But it was just the two of them. Danielle patted Baby Bump in a way that she hoped was reassuring and smiled.

Danielle realized Simon had never been in this classroom before. His eyes darted around the room. It was pretty hard not to. Every available inch was papered with kids' poster paint artwork.

Still patting her belly, she smiled at him encouragingly, like his hand had shot up and waved around.

"It's pretty green," he said.

"Well, the children wanted to paint frogs. It took on a life of its own. They did a lot of them at home and brought them in."

"Dan, what happened?"

"Nothing happened. That's the worst of it. Nothing happens. Over and over. You're right, I can't continue in the classroom. Not without accommodation, and that cavalry isn't arriving."

"So it's over?"

Danielle shrugged. "I need a ride home. It turns out that Nothing can happen on a school bus."

Simon crossed the room and took his wife in his arms. Danielle shuddered in his embrace, silently weeping. Pregnancy.

"The worst of it," she said gasping breath, "The worst is there's nobody. Nobody to take over," her voice broke, "the tadpoles."

"We'll figure out something."

"About half of them have back legs," said Danielle, gently disentangling herself. "The kids figured out that the ones crowded into the little tank matured faster. At least they think so. This afternoon I was going to teach them how to graph change so that they could see it day by day."

Danielle opened a desk drawer and took out her purse. She looked around as if there were things she needed to take with her but couldn't remember what. As if to remind her, she felt her baby kick.

"And another thing they figured out. All on their own. Complete surprise to me. Those big webbed swimming legs? They work just fine, so you'd think they'd rocket those pollywogs around. But Mrs. Milner's Second Grade has news for you. Tadpoles *hate* having back legs. They slow them down. Tadpoles move by wriggling. They can't figure out what to do with those rear legs. They just get in the way."

Her friend Pam Gillett poked her nose in at the door. "I've got them all afternoon. Not to worry."

"Nautical disasters?" said Danielle. It was an in-joke, citing a hypothetical foolproof emergency curriculum.

"Mary Celeste. The Flying Dutchman. Titanic. Their little fannies will be glued to their chairs."

"Hey," Pam turned to Simon, as if solving a one-of-these-things-is-different-than-the-others quiz. "We met before. You're the husband, right? Did Danielle buzz you in?"

"No need. I'm on the vetted list," Simon said.

"How's that?" said Pam.

Simon replied, "Last fall I was setting up air quality monitors to address some parent's concern. Out of an abundance of caution. It required me being here during the school day. You know, to measure air exchange when there were actually people in the building. So they ran background on me."

"That's interesting," said Pam Gillett. She turned to her friend and whispered to her just loud enough for Simon to overhear. "Danielle, twist his arm. Seriously. It would only be for another two weeks. Maybe three. He could be your accommodation."

"Her what?" said Simon.

"Accommodation. It's what the school is required to give you if you need one. To continue doing your job. Compliance with the ADA."

"ADA? I don't get it. I'm not a wheelchair ramp. I'm not a sign language interpreter. I'm not even a qualified note taker. I have no relevant training. I'm an electrical contractor."

"What Danielle needs accommodation for is that she may unexpectedly be absent during the school day. Seems to me the only relevant accommodation for absence is presence. You could be present. For her, for the students, to keep everybody safe and secure."

"Like an emotional support animal?" said Simon.

"Teacher's pet," said Pam Gillett.

"Very funny," said Simon. "So I'd sit at a little desk in the back and wait for something to happen?"

"Absolutely not. That would just be creepy and unsettling. The children need to know that you're a helper. So you'd have to be helping."

"But I'm not a teaching assistant. I'm vetted to be around school children, not to work with them."

"Simon's right," said Danielle. "Thank you, Pam, for trying, but even if Simon was willing and could get the time off work, I don't see how we could justify having him in the classroom doing nothing. Let alone charging by the hour for it."

Simon went over and peered into the big aquarium. He watched a tadpole futilely lashing its tail and dragging its hind legs behind, like an amphibian built by a committee.

"So. What happens next," said Simon.

"I'd have to file for an immediate leave of absence. They'd bring in a substitute teacher. And I'd have to find some way to explain it to the children." Danielle gestured at the dozens of poster paint green pictures of widemouthed smiling frogs. "Give them some kind of closure."

Danielle knew enough about substitute teachers to know that it was basically crowd control and rote worksheets to meet statewide standards. No way would a sub take on the challenging chaos of twenty-nine small wriggling creatures in metamorphosis.

Pam Gillett stood between Mrs. Milner and the door. "You're pregnant. Every woman on the faculty who's been there knows it by now. The men don't have a clue. Do you have any idea what kind of power that gives you? No administrator, no *male* administrator, is going to go up against that. Use it, Dan."

"No," said Simon, continuing to stare into the tank. "I mean what's next for the tadpoles? Front legs?"

"Symmetry," said Danielle. "The children and I were going to see if both front legs develop at the exact same time, or if one side develops before the other. Jumping off from that, we'd be looking for all kinds of symmetries. Bilateral. Mirror. Maybe even Handedness."

"And the week after?"

Simon just didn't get it. When she walked out that door it was over. If Miss Praeger took over her section, she'd view this whole amphibian thing as unsanitary, at best. Call the custodian. She'd never notice, let alone explore with the students the implications of five rear toes but only four front ones.

"Then the froglet absorbs its tail. Whatever the substitute says, it doesn't fall off. Re-absorbed. How does an animal reabsorb part of himself? Fascinating to watch. We'll put a dot of dye on the tip and see where it goes. Then the best part. The jumping. If you've swum all your life, how do you learn to jump?"

"How indeed?" said Pam Gillett. "What could that possibly feel like?" She gestured at her friend's swelling belly. "The children could write stories, talk about past and future. Why starting something new is difficult and scary. And why it's worth it. God, Danielle, it's the perfect Second Grade assignment! I wish I could take all of this over." Pam Gillet heard the sound of restive students in her room across the hall. "Unfortunately," she said in departure, "Not an option."

"Nautical disasters!" Danielle called after her.

Simon stepped up to the teacher's desk and tried to heft the big aquarium. He was barely able to budge it, moving it to the edge of the desk. "I need you to be really honest with me right now," said Simon. "How bad are the seizures?"

"I got scared. It's not that they're bad. It's just that I got a cluster. A cascade. And suddenly the future looked too dangerous to face alone."

"You're not alone," said Simon.

"You know what I mean. I have to think about what's best for our child, for Baby Bump. And if I can be there for all these young artists," she gestured around at the frog paintings. And then, in an emphatic whisper, "and scientists."

"We're going to see this baby through together. Promise made, promise kept," said Simon.

He again braced himself and wrapped his arms around the slippery sides of the big tank. He lifted it clear of the desktop. Then set it down again, back in the center of the desk.

"It looks to me like you haven't thought this through," said Simon. "I'm talking about jumping. I don't see how these aquariums are going to contain froglets—or whatever they're called—once they learn to jump."

"Screen lids."

"No way. One of these leggy guys is going to ricochet himself off that screen until he knocks it loose. Then all the others are going to follow after."

Looking down into the tank, Danielle watched a pollywog doing a breaststroke kick across the water surface, having apparently learned what hind legs are for.

"When these tadpoles become real official frogs what they're going to need is accommodations. A whole amphibian environment. A baby frog nursery. That's something I can build. I can do it during the school day. The kids can help me with plans and suggestions. And maybe they'll learn a little about carpentry and construction. Something useful."

"I'm sure there are rules against that, too," said Danielle.

"Let's find out who has the brass to try and stop us," Simon said.

Navigation

A book should contain pure discoveries, glimpses of terra firma, *though by shipwrecked mariners, and not the art of navigation by those who have never been out of sight of land.*

Henry David Thoreau

Chapter 1

When we were children we took long walks in the woods. My kid sister would say "Lewis, let's go to the big tree in the clearing where we can climb up and see for a thousand thousand miles!" And then Alice would lead me there. I could never find the big tree by myself. I relied upon my kid sister to find it for us. She could always find it. And the pool where the tadpoles swam in the shallows. And the place where we buried the treasure. And the way back home.

But big brothers and little sisters grow in different directions. Soon childhood made me fiercely independent. I strode proudly aloof into those familiar woods, a latter-day Thoreau, to commune with my own deep and incommunicable thoughts. And I promptly got lost. Not just a little lost. As profoundly bewildered as my self-importance would allow me to admit. I felt like Daniel Boone, who never admitted to being lost, but allowed that he had been a "mite perplexed" in the woods for several days.

It's not that I wasn't paying attention. I had grown up with these trees and streams, back fences and wildflowers, and all of it held my attention, each small detail. I knew exactly where I was. The problem was I didn't know what was next to where I was. There was simply no map in my head that would lead me home. Or anywhere else, for that matter.

Hours passed wandering in what obviously were circles, since the same landmarks kept appearing again and again. I spotted neighbors watching me with puzzled expressions as I crossed and recrossed their backyards. A Lewis without a Clark. I skirted along fences to gates and gaps. Was our house on this side of the Timsons, or the other side?

Then my sister Alice found me and guided me home. She pretended that she hadn't come looking for me. I pretended that I didn't need her help at all. The whole way home I lectured her in the finer points of woodcraft, how moss grows thicker on the north sides of trees.

Finding north-facing moss remained a theoretical pursuit, but my troubles with navigation were very real, and were not limited to the woods. The spatial sequence of streets, stores, school hallways, even our own house didn't etch any kind of recognizable pattern into my memory and had to be learned by rote. When our parents repainted the interior walls, I was a mite perplexed, stumbling upon kitchen, bedroom, bathroom entirely by chance, until I had incorporated the new sequence of colors into my memory.

Let's face it, it's not just anyone who can get lost on a baseball diamond. I was a pretty good batter; I had a natural's eye on the ball. But in my short career as a sandlot hero, the cheers turned almost immediately to groans of disbelief. I would hit a single and then run to third base. Which has always been against the rules. And I've been on second and stolen first. Which, curiously, was completely legal until the 1920s when it was banned for "making a travesty of the game." The one time I actually hit one over the fence I couldn't find my way home. I made a wrong turn at third base and sprinted into the outfield along the foul line. Eventually they found the ball in the weeds and tagged me out in what was deemed a mercy killing.

Apart from my kid sister, Alice, no one quite believed that I got so easily lost. My truancy got labeled with every other possible explanation. My mother said I was dreamy, absent-minded, living in my own world. Actually, I was living in a world that was utterly not my own. My father thought I was willfully vagrant, deliberately not going to the place I was supposed to be when I was supposed to be there. When I was late to supper, I went without supper.

I had tried drawing maps. Not, of course, real maps. Real maps look like how God sees the world. Always directly above every place, everywhere all at the same time. People can't see the world that way. Not even pilots or astronauts. It simply isn't possible.

Because real maps made no sense, I started to map my world in a way that did make sense: Start where I am. Then draw the next place, right next to it. Then the place after that, sketched in lockstep sequence. The result was a long ribbon of places, each next to the other. I later learned that this was a *periplus*, an itinerary of proximate landmarks, the way ancient navigators found their way along a coastline. A little bit like the way that AAA used to send Airstream trailers across the country, navigating by Triptik.

There was one serious problem with the maps I made. Pretty soon they ran off the edge of a sheet of paper. I considered writing them out on a spool of adding machine tape, but this seemed awkward. Then I realized that drawing my proximities in a spiral worked just as well as writing them in one long straight line. And used a lot less paper. If where I'm standing is on my spiral map, I could usually find the next place and spiral in or out from place to place. But if I stepped off the spiral, all hope in paper was lost. As was I.

I knew that real maps didn't look anything like my spiral maps. Real maps viewed the world from God's point of view. And that requires you to orient yourself to the map. And then it requires you to orient the map to the terrain. In other words, you have to know where you are in order to figure out where you are.

There are streets and rivers and towns on real maps. But I can't find myself anywhere on those maps. And nobody else is on the map either. I have had nightmares about this. In my dreams God sees all the roads and rivers in the world but doesn't see the people. For Him the people don't exist. From time to time a new road appears, and God takes note of it. But that's all He sees of humanity. Like we are burrowing beetles that leave our tracks on the underside of bark.

ॐ

I went on my first real date with Becky Rosen. I was a freshman in high school, she was a year older than me; her parents had loaned her the car. Down the block from our house, she stopped the car and told me that I should drive. I only had my learner's permit, so strictly speaking this wasn't legal. But I really wanted Becky to like me, so I came around and got behind the wheel. She slid over as close to me as seats and shoulder harnesses would allow. I adjusted the rearview mirror like I'd been doing it all my life. And pulled out smoothly into the non-traffic.

The stated plan was to go to the multiplex to see a movie and then come right home. The actual plan was more complicated, since no part of it was actually stated. I was the driver. I was supposed to know where to go and what to do. When we reached the corner, I turned left. That was my first mistake.

Three hours later Becky drove me home. She said she didn't mind missing the movie, so I don't think that was the problem. I'm not sure, but I think the problem was that we never stopped driving. I tried to kiss her when she stopped in front of my house. She said, "You've got to be kidding, right?"

☙

Many years have passed since then. They say a broken bone grows back stronger at the place of fracture. That may be why when it was time to choose my thesis project, I chose computational navigation. Without getting too geeky on you, the basic idea is that the hare knows where the finish line is. But there are many ways to get to the finish line. In fact, many *optimal* ways of getting there. To choose the best route to run, he has to determine what "best" is. And that's a complex calculation because each leg of the journey has its own optimal calculations. Like a chess game, the options soon spiral beyond any reasonable arithmetic. Which leaves the hare frozen on the starting blocks.

The tortoise doesn't have this problem. He just puts one foot in front of the other. It doesn't really matter if he is going in the "right" direction or the "wrong" one. He is moving, and by being in motion he collapses the set of possibilities so that the best route is fairly easily arrived at. As long as he never goes to the same place twice. You just subtract where you've been from where you're going by knowing precisely where you aren't. That, at least, is the theory.

What kept me awake night after night at the Computing Center was that the hares kept outrunning the tortoises. I had to build a better tortoise. This was something that I knew I could do. I'd had a lifetime of practice.

I was navigating across the campus, trying to pay attention to my spiral map, when a V-shaped flock of Canada geese noisily crossed the sky, causing me to lose my place. I had learned that when this happens to stand absolutely still until you can relocate yourself in the spiral. Moving even a couple of steps can change the angle, make the landmarks unrecognizable. But I needed to see those geese. As I watched, the goose in the lead stopped leading. He fell back into the flock and another goose took over. And I thought: Does every goose in the flight know exactly where they're going? Or do they only know *approximately*, and each new leader adjusts the last one's best guess with his own? I needed to know where they were going, how they were getting there. I stepped out of the spiral.

When I finally found the Zoology Building that housed Ornithology, hours later, all of the offices were closed for the day. There was no one to ask about the geese. Then I noticed one lab was still lit. One female graduate student was hunched over a stereo microscope, busy dissecting what turned out to be bird brains. The silken waterfall of brown hair that tumbled to her shoulders swayed ever so slightly with her small precise motions.

I waited quietly until she finished. But she didn't finish. I felt foolish and considered leaving her uninterrupted in her scholarly pursuit. The geese weren't that important. But then there was the problem of how I was going to get home from here. I really needed her to point me in the right direction, or I'd likely spend the whole night wandering the campus. So I cleared my throat.

She got up slowly from her chair. Assuming that I am an excellent judge of feminine beauty (from a distance) she was, in my estimation, radiant. Luminous, with an element of intriguing.

She stepped away from the swivel chair, which continued to rotate a few degrees. She pivoted to face me. Our eyes met. Her feet were planted in a low, wide stance, her knees flexed. Her hands transformed to lethal weapons, poised for action. She growled at me, "Get lost."

I ran out of Zoology as quickly as I could find an exit. Outside, I realized that I had to get away from the entrance. What if she came out and I was standing next to the building? I didn't want to scare her further. Who knows what kind of bodily harm she might inflict? I put my right hand on the side of the building and walked, sliding my palm along the bricks until I ran into a loading dock. I took a deep breath and detached from the building. I started to navigate home.

It was fortunate that the moon was nearly full. I needed its light to draw my spiral map from the Zoology Building back to my student apartment. Drawing the map slowed my progress to a turtle's crawl, but I wanted to have that map. And it gave me time to consider the mathematical theory known as "the drunkard's walk." A drunk leaves his home and walks an arbitrary distance in a straight line, then turns at an arbitrary angle. If he keeps doing this, it is a mathematical certainty (probability=1) that he will find his way home. Sooner or later. Of course, this is a mathematical drunk, not a real drunk. A real drunk walks much more like me. But drunks don't sketch maps as they stumble around.

Consider a graph, one axis running from conventionally beautiful to enticingly exotic, the other axis spanning from voluptuously sensual to regally aloof. In the exact center of that graph is a graduate student in ornithology.

Lewis, you've fallen off the map. I stood absolutely still, as I'd taught myself to do, staring at the last notation on the spiral, then slowly turned in a circle, hoping to spot my last landmark. I got lucky.

ˏˎ

The next morning I followed an old spiral map to the flagpole. The flagpole was not a destination, but I had circled it on the paper. Because when I reached the flagpole, I could jump to my new map and spiral back to Zoology from there. I drew a straight red line across the spiral to that point, cutting out several unnecessary gyres.

In the lobby a bulletin board displayed photos of all the Zoology faculty, and (fortunately) the teaching assistants as well. Her name was Robin. Same hair, same eyes, same lips. The photo confirmed what I suspected. She is like the number 28. Break it up into its divisors: 1, 2, 4, 7, 14. Then add up these products of division. The self adds up to itself again, the miraculous sum of all of her parts. A quality so mathematically rare that it has its own name: Perfect.

I do well in academic surroundings. All of the doors in academic buildings are numbered. I found Robin's office without recourse to mapmaking. She wasn't in. So I waited in the hallway across from the reassuring number. Another TA who shared the office did appear eventually and unlocked the door. I asked him when Robin would be in, but he had no idea. I asked him what "as the crow flies" meant, ornithologically. But he was a Scandinavian foreign student studying fish populations. So he had no clue.

He had no objection to my waiting, so I waited. I brought some journal abstracts to read, though I can't say I made much headway with them. I was anxious. I was significantly less than certain that Robin would respond well to my appearance in her office. After the incident of the night before, an apology was in order. And if that went well, an explanation.

I got out one of my teaching assistant business cards and held it in my right hand as I waited, so that would be the first thing she'd see. That seemed non-threatening.

Several other faculty lecturers arrived, but not Robin. When they had conferences with undergraduates, I stood out in the hallway expecting her footsteps, my business card turning limp in my hand. She never showed up. Finally, Sven had to lock up for the evening. He turned out to be a nice guy, though a little too invested in the future of fish for my taste. Before he closed the tiny windowless office, I jotted a few words on my card and left it on Robin's desk.

As we exited the building, I asked him where he was going. He looked at me a bit funny, then said he was going to Merriweather for supper. I said that was near graduate housing. But I knew I didn't have a map on me for Merriweather and I had learned the hard way that the word "near" was treacherous. So I asked him if he would walk me to my apartment. I could actually see him going through his English vocabulary trying to find the right terminology. He wanted to refuse my apparent sexual overture, but without being offensive. Like I said, he was Scandinavian. I reassured him that my motives were innocent, that it was just a national custom. It's an American tradition to walk total strangers back to their domiciles.

ൠ

I tried to put Robin out of my mind that night. But that was a bit like trying not to think about a rhinoceros when someone tells you not to think about rhinoceroses. Not that I'm comparing Robin to a rhinoceros. I'm just saying that I did a whole lot more thinking than sleeping. Mostly I was thinking how I had done absolutely everything wrong. Spending the day in her office would probably be seen as creepy. Leaving the business card wasn't such a hot idea. And Sven would no doubt describe me as an odd duck, assuming that his grasp of English idiom included that phrase.

In the morning, I very pointedly put the Zoology Building spiral in my Inactive file. I had already made a fool of myself in front of at least two people there in what amounted to a wild goose chase. I would go to my own building and work on my tortoise. I would give anything in Life Sciences a wide berth for the indefinite future.

It wasn't a good day at the office. Euler's Seven Bridges of Königsberg proof wasn't getting me anywhere. The hare, who could repeat himself and cross the same bridge twice, was beating the tortoise, who couldn't. Winning every single race, as usual. I tried at least a dozen variations on tortoise. None of them helped. Making the tortoise remember everything just made him slower. Allowing him, mathematically, to forget his oldest mistakes, his "wrong" turns, didn't make him any more hare-like, it just made him more tentative. The poor beast was just standing with one foot raised, with every move looking like the wrong one. For one dark hour I actually tried to handicap the hare, to give myself some kind of victory, even a false one.

I had just, algorithmically speaking, ripped the left hind leg off the hare when she showed up. She knocked resolutely on my cubicle. I whirled around fearful that it was my thesis advisor about to catch me in the act of dismemberment. It was Robin. Holding my business card. The campus police were not with her.

"I just want to know what this means," she said. "You come lurking around my lab late at night and stand behind me for half an hour, scaring the bejesus out of me. And then you spend the entire next day stalking me in my office." Her feet moved into a wide balanced stance. "Then when Sven finally kicks you out, you leave this." Her knees flexed. "What the hell kind of joke is this?"

She was absolutely radiant. Had Lewis known that making a woman angry would make a woman more beautiful, Lewis would have made all women angry. This is a false syllogism. And when the woman knows martial arts, a dangerous one. Her knees flexed again.

"It actually means just what it says," I said lamely. "You told me to get lost."

"So you wrote on the card 'I got lost'. But you didn't. You turned up at my office. You hung out in my office. All day. And when you finally left, you left this. Are you trying to be funny?"

"No. It's just the truth. I did get lost. I came to your lab to ask directions. And when you chased me away, I got lost." That wasn't exactly the truth, but it was pretty close to the truth. "For about six hours."

Her knees unflexed. "What?"

"I spent the hours between 10:00pm and 4:00am trying to get from the Zoology Building to the Sunnyside Apartments."

"But that's a 20-minute walk."

"For some people."

"Look, don't expect me to feel sorry for you if you were wandering around drunk all night."

"I wasn't drunk. It's just. Well, it's just the way I'm wired."

"And what is that supposed to mean?" said Robin.

So I explained. "All of us are somewhere on the May-Britt Moser spectrum. That's why some people have a natural gift for navigation, and why some people are directionally impaired. It's brain architecture, grid cell neurons. It has to do with the hippocampus, a little piece of the brain shaped like a seahorse." Robin took a chair. "I just happen to be on the extreme end of the spectrum. The extremely lost end of the spectrum."

"So you can't," she said.

"Find my way out of a paper bag."

Robin laughed. Had Lewis known that making this woman laugh would make this woman even more beautiful, Lewis would always make this woman laugh.

ଔ

I explained my navigation project to her. The whole tortoise and hare business. I left out the Markov chain algorithms. You have to hold something back, for later. I kept expecting to see that glazed-over look. She didn't glaze. She just told me I was wrong.

"Listen, I think you've got the wrong idea about rabbits. The rabbit doesn't take the shortest path to the finish line. Just like a bird doesn't take the shortest migration route. Or a student doesn't take the shortest shortcut across campus. They take the shortest path that they already know. They are in haste to get someplace, but they are in an even greater flurry to not get lost. Fear constrains them to only familiar routes," said Robin. "The tortoise blazes unfamiliar trails."

"That makes the tortoise sound positively heroic."

"Well, he is. He doesn't have any choice in the matter. So he's heroic."

"That's paradoxical."

"Very observant of you." Robin took my hand. Her hands were warm holding mine. The following transcription is of only limited reliability owing to that fact.

"Say you put your tortoise and your hare in a maze," said Robin. "The hare knows that the exit is on the far side of the maze, so he immediately goes in that direction. But what we know about mazes is that the direct path is almost never the correct path. The tortoise takes whatever path he comes to first, because he doesn't know which way to go."

It was my turn to correct her. "Not exactly. The tortoise knows where he started from. So he takes the path that's least likely to bring him back to where he started. The tortoise makes lots of mistakes, falls short of the mark. But he remembers where he has been and doesn't repeat his errors. The hare has forgotten all about the starting line, his only aim is to reach his goal. So when the rabbit arrives back at the starting point he hasn't learned anything. He's just more frustrated."

"Some days being a lagomorph simply doesn't pay."

Lagomorph? So long as Robin kept holding my hand, she could say anything and I would nod in agreement.

"There's this thing about martial arts," said Robin, apropos of nothing. "The sensei shows you the form. He takes you through it and you practice the form. With practice you get better at it. Until you stop getting better. Then my teacher does something unexpected. He has us sit on the mat. And he tells us a story. After he finishes telling the story we sit silent for a while until we finish taking it in. Then we do the form again. And the form is always improved. Because now we better understand who is practicing the form.

"This is the story he told last week: *A Zen monk carried water every day from the spring up the steep trail to the monastery. He had a shoulder yoke to carry the water with two big pots, one on either end. The pot on the left side was a good solid pot that arrived at its destination brimming with water. The pot on the right side had a crack in it, so that it dribbled out water and arrived only half full. All the other monks complained about the lack of water and pestered him to fix the cracked pot. But he never would. Finally, the Master asked the monk why he refused to repair the water pot. The monk said that he didn't want his fellow monks to go thirsty. The Master said, that's exactly why you should patch that pot. No, replied the monk, when I started carrying water the spring was hard to find. I often got lost and the monks often went thirsty waiting for my water. With time I learned the path to the spring. But I will grow old and die, and another monk will have to fetch water from the spring. So I will not patch the pot. The flawed pot drips water all along the right side of the path. And where the water drips, wildflowers have sprung up the length of the path. The way is marked with beauty. That beauty will live after me and refresh thirsty monks after I am gone."*

"That is probably the nicest possible way of calling me a crackpot," I said.

"Perfection is highly overrated."

"Tell that to my thesis advisor."

"All of us are more-or-less cracked pots, harboring unseen perfections in our imperfections," she said. "Some of us get to be water carrier monks who recognize the virtue of those imperfections. And a lucky few of us get to be wildflowers. I think that's what love is."

I am a 23-year-old graduate student in applied mathematics. I am a field of flowers in bloom.

ෲ

It didn't happen that evening. Or two days later on what might be considered our First Date, which we spent in a revival screening of Hitchcock's "The Birds." Robin's choice. As date movies go, I don't recommend it. It may start out like a screwball romantic comedy, but don't be fooled. In fact, it's terrifying. Real nightmare stuff. But Robin held my hand throughout, and that was enough for me to see the romance at the heart of it all: Boy meets girl. Boy loses girl. Gull attacks girl. Boy finds girl and tenderly applies bandages. Crows gather menacingly in children's playground. Boy and girl go on a date to a restaurant—and are assaulted by a lot more seagulls. Gas station bursts into flames. Boy loses girl, again. Boy rescues girl from phone booth as birds smash against the glass walls all around her. Boy and girl drive off together into the sunset. Evacuated by the National Guard. Roll credits.

Somehow Robin seemed unperturbed by the whole ghastly assault of bludgeoning wings and eye-gouging beaks. I suspect she had seen it more than once before and wasn't rooting for Tippi Hedren. I'd only heard about it. When I wasn't closing my eyes and wincing, I was quietly rooting for Rod Taylor. Love always triumphs in the end. Or at least it ought to.

In a coffeeshop after the movie, Robin explained that this 1963 movie was Hitchcock's inspired response to Rachel Carson's 1962 *Silent Spring*. Hitchcock somehow knew that a viable environmental movement would have to draw its energy not from elegiac sadness, but from visceral fear. When we least expected it, Nature would do to us what we had done to Her. I kept an eye on the plate glass windows and leapt just a little bit every time the barista steamed a cappuccino.

For our Second Date, Robin picked me up with her car and took us to a steak house restaurant. This surprised me. Somehow, I had imagined she was a vegetarian. As it turned out she eats everything, except birds. I don't think there's even a name for that.

Our dinner conversation circled around the subject of species extinction, like slowly draining water. Every time I tried to change the topic, Robin pulled us back into the death spiral of Carolina Parakeets, Great Auks, Passenger Pigeons, and Ivory-billed Woodpeckers. I felt personally implicated in the 19th century millenary trade in exotic plumage. My sirloin tasted of Dodo grease. As you do when you start to feel the nausea born of vertigo, I looked directly into her eyes. Her eyes were wise. I don't know how else to put it. They were lovely and warm and wise.

This tale of the Termination of Species was what she needed to say. It wasn't weird or obsessive or depressive, it was just her saying to me what we all know. And choose never to talk about. She was trusting me with something in her that wasn't light and easy and sparkly.

I told her she was right to feel this way. And meant it. She was.

She started in on the California Condor. Then, in mid-sentence, she stopped. And she winked at me.

"Lewis. When I find myself not being very likeable, you somehow continue to like me."

"That's because I don't like you." (In for a dime, in for a dollar) "I love you."

Puck does his gentle love mischief with the nectar of a flower dripped in sleepers' eyes. Winged Cupid uses a razor-sharp arrow.

"Tell your thesis advisor you got a solid B+," she winked at me again. "Now let's talk about something more pleasant. Like whether you need to be anywhere important tomorrow morning."

Robin drove us back to her apartment. She led me by the hand through several intervening rooms that I have no recollection of at all, into the bedroom. I had no trouble finding my way after that.

ভ

I awoke with the morning sun to find this exquisite woman warmly asleep beside me. Her beauty took my breath away. Her breath had the deep regularity of someone who has no intentions of being awake any time soon. Her rich brown hair spread like a cloud across her pillow. Rumpled in beautiful disarray, wisps in a confusing confliction of directions. The weather of my life had changed overnight. I was lost in the intricacy of her hair. And I had to pee.

Our visions of romance never include this salient fact. To be wide awake in an unfamiliar apartment, and to have to pee. And to have not the faintest idea where the bathroom is.

I ever-so-gently slipped out the side of the bed and grabbed the minimal necessary clothing. I opened the door. It was Robin's closet. I closed it again.

Fortunately, there was only one other door, and that led me to the hallway. Which presented a series of doors. One of them was likely the bathroom. The others could very likely be the bedrooms of sleeping housemates. For all I knew, I could open a door on Sven in his bedroom dreaming of schooling fish, awakening to my half-undressed state and my naked excuses. I sent forth a prayer to Cupid and all the gods of lovers that the bathroom door was left ajar. Through some miracle it was.

Cupid had been kind. But he's just a boy, with a boy's sense of humor. I had closed Robin's door behind me. And now I didn't know what door I had so recently come from. I should have counted my steps. Or hung a sock on the doorknob. But I hadn't thought of those things. And now I was shivering in the corridor with a choice of three doors.

I considered waiting in the hallway until someone emerged from one of the doors. I could go back to the bathroom and drape myself like an ancient Roman in bath towels. Two or three towels to increase bodily warmth and decrease the amount of Lewis on view. It would no doubt look pretty silly. But in my terrycloth toga I could wait indefinitely for a door to open.

But, assuming that all three were bedroom doors, the odds were against me. One chance in three that Robin would be first to emerge. And find me in a state that might cause her to question her judgment of the night before. Two chances in three that I would be face to face with someone who didn't expect me and would likely not appreciate me in their hallway. In their towel.

When logic and memory fail, you just have to trust to something you can't quantify. The turtle knows where he isn't. The turtledove somehow senses where he needs to land. Before I had a chance to second-guess myself, I walked to a door and turned the handle.

I count myself among the luckiest of men.

ᴄ8

I had to ask her about it sooner or later. It turned out to be sooner. I asked. "Is there a particular reason why you don't, you know, eat birds? As a dietary restriction, I don't think that there's even a name for that. I know how fond you are of birds. Still, you don't seem to have any problem dissecting their brains."

"Which," Robin responded, "inevitably involves them being quite entirely dead. Moral high ground it's not. Science, in my estimation, is sufficient justification; chicken nuggets are not. So I don't eat birds. On principle."

"But you eat steak. And bacon. And hamburgers and ham."

"I do. Our appetites for mammals are pretty much the same. But neither of us would ever eat cats or dogs or horses. And you, Lewis, are pretty squeamish about the fact that Peruvians eat guinea pigs. I think you had one as a child."

"I suppose all of us meat eaters are pretty morally ambiguous."

"I'm not. *Aves* is a well-defined class of creatures. Which I don't eat. And I make no exceptions."

I felt like I was getting nowhere in this getting-to-know-her conversation.

I tried to find another way to say 'why?' "So you've picked birds as your preferred taxonomy? One small step closer to moral purity? Like giving something up for Lent?"

"No. Arbitrary it's not. Listen, just because it's not a common social construct doesn't mean it isn't ethical," said Robin, looking a bit more annoyed with me than I had intended. "*Some* people have a hard time with the fact that the crow cawing on the branch is smarter than Fido on the leash."

"People don't eat crow."

"The general principle applies."

"OK." I looked around for a change of subjects, but nothing presented itself.

"Lewis. You know the word 'bovine' don't you? It describes a state of placid mindlessness. The absence of thinking, caring, creatively interacting with the world around. Cows are bovine. Calves are not bovine. They frisk, they play, they explore. Then they become cows. Sheep do the same thing. Lambs are alive to the world. By the time they become sheep, they're little more than mechanisms responding to a handful of pretty obvious fears and desires. One dog can push a hundred around. They act just like sheep.

"One of the great secrets of science is that all of those lab experiments on learning and problem solving, all of those mice in mazes, are immature mice. All of our studies of mammal intelligence are done with very young animals. We get better results that way.

"I've seen this in every mammal I've come across. They start out full of intelligence. They have to, in order to survive to reproductive age. Then they become placid. They end up so inured to habit that eating them hardly raises a qualm."

I had some qualms about eating the dull. But I didn't interrupt her.

"Birds don't do that. Is an old crow any less inquisitive than a young crow? Does the vocabulary of an old parrot shrink? It's the opposite. Because birds don't grow up. Why? Because they migrate. They pick up and move, often thousands of miles through unimaginable hazards. And then they turn around and return, often to the exact same place. Return to re-establish territory and define its perimeters with interactive song. Return to build a new nest in a new tree, which presents entirely new architectural problems. Because they migrate, birds continue to inquire and investigate and form complex and passionate relationships with other members of their species. That, in itself, is enough to exempt them from my bill of fare."

I should have left well enough alone. But there were holes in her argument that you could drive a herd of caribou through. "Chickens don't migrate."

"And maybe you can teach an old dog new tricks," she replied. "In nature there are always multiple exceptions to every generality. And things get even murkier when we introduce domestication into the mix. Nature is full of contradictions. But that doesn't mean we have to be. People who eat no higher on the vertebrate tree than fish don't inquire whether salmon are smarter than flounder. They make a rule for themselves and stick with it.

"I like the way birds approach the world," she continued. "They're intensely emotive and absolutely pragmatic. They're far more visual than mammals and more colorful. And they employ a grand and subtle spectrum of singing sounds. They don't grunt and they don't snuffle."

"And they can find their way," I said. Perhaps the irony was lost on her.

⋘

I brought Robin home to meet my parents. Or rather, Robin brought me, since I didn't own a car. Not that I can't drive. I actually love to drive. To rapidly traverse space feels victorious, putting wings on a tortoise. Going 55 miles an hour is an intoxicating feeling. Trees and signs and underpasses whip by, with not the slightest need to write them down. A highway is a straight line. With numbered exits.

Robin let me drive the highway portion of the route. She seemed relaxed, there in the passenger seat, the incomprehensible road map lying so casually across her lap. I wanted to put my head out the window like a dog and let the wind flap my ears. "Hawk!" I called out as we passed.

"*Buteo jamaicensis!*" Robin sang back to the red-tail surveying its roadside realm from the top of a tree. And then, suddenly as seen, gone from view.

The one thing I don't like about driving is changing lanes. Not the traffic part of it. The traffic part is fine. I have no problem with proximity. The trouble with changing lanes is that the highway looked different when you change lanes. You use your blinker, check the mirrors, slide over. Then you panic inside. Were you still on the same road? Had you somehow taken a lefthand exit? Where the hell were you?! Staying in the right-hand lane works best for me. Three crows crossing overhead. So long as the right-hand lane doesn't peel away to an exit. That's really quite unfair.

I pulled over, we changed seats, and Robin drove the last leg of the journey, the suburban streets fading off into wooded cul de sacs. She stopped every couple of blocks to consult the map. I did my best to be helpful. "That looks familiar," I said. "We must be getting close." Finally, she pulled the car to a halt. "Is this the house?" I looked at the shingles, the window shutters, the trees, the flagstone path to the door, the unfamiliar rose bush. "It looks 85% like home."

My mother greeted us at the door. She gave me a hug. She said I looked too thin. She gave Robin a hug. She complimented Robin on her clothing. Robin complimented Mother on her jewelry. Mother complimented Robin on her punctuality. Robin complimented Mother on her gardens. I wondered what that rose bush was doing there.

"Lewis, I can't wait to show you what I've collected for you," said mother as she breezed us into the house. I followed, keeping her in sight at all times. We emerged into the living room. Dad was just standing up from his chair, the book he was reading splayed open on the upholstered arm.

"Ah, the prodigal son arrives," said Dad, extending his hands into something awkwardly halfway between a handshake and an embrace. "Great to have you home. And you must be…"

"Robin."

"First sign of spring." He shook her hand. "Great son, great." I started to relax. Father approved of Robin. God knows what Dad was expecting. A girl who looked like a chewed #2 pencil with a head of pink-dyed hair like an overused eraser?

Robin complimented Dad on his living room.

"Here it is," said Mother, holding the file folder labeled 'Lewis' with both hands. "I've been working on this one for years. Then just last week it all came together. Come see."

It was another installment of Mother's Lost and Found. In preparation for the visit I had tried to explain the Lost and Found to Robin. Mother's habit of collecting and organizing clippings from newspapers and magazines. "It sounds artistic," said Robin. "It's obsessive/compulsive," I said. "The pot calling the kettle black," she replied.

This visit's installment of the L & F was entitled *Unexpected Vistas*. Mother had collected descriptions of sudden panoramas. The first sighting of Machu Picchu. And Lhasa. Coming through the tunnel to see Pittsburgh spread out before you. The vivid green of the infield at Fenway Park. The atrium garden at the Isabella Stewart Gardner. Lewis and Clark reaching the Pacific. Brigham Young's vision of the Great Salt Lake. The descriptions were beautiful, they wrung poetry from journalism. Robin read a few aloud, to Mother's obvious approval.

But I knew it wasn't just a folder full of clippings. That was the bait in the trap. Mother's organizational scheme was relentless. Each clipping was pencil marked in the margins.

"Look," she said, picking up an account of crossing the Nevada desert at night to Las Vegas. "There's a rhythm here of expectation and arrival. These people *find* some place. They don't know what to expect and then they *find* it. I've marked a little arrow next to each one. And here's another one just like that." She piled the two together, like a successful move at solitaire. "I've been trying to decide whether those belong together. What do you think, Lewis?"

A rather long time later, Mother excused herself to the kitchen, leaving us with the clippings. Not too long after that, dinner was served.

Dad started the table conversation with one of his office war stories. A major Swedish furniture company (whose name he couldn't disclose) was bringing out a new line of birch furniture. But they were using wood fasteners with the camber and unthreaded shank length for oak. Needless to say, things were not going well. Father is a screw engineer. So far as I know, he has never found anything funny about that.

After things were set to rights in the furniture world, Dad turned to Robin. "So. What is it you do?" Mother shot him a look. "I mean, study?"

"I work with bird brains," said Robin. Father slapped the table, convulsed with laughter. "Me too," he managed to choke out.

We ate in silence for a long while. "Robin," I said, "tell them about the flock/territory switch."

"OK." She began tentatively. "Birds, especially male birds, have two opposed behavioral repertoires. They are either establishing territory, or they are flocking." Mother nodded encouragingly, glancing back and forth at her two male birds at the table. "This is an oversimplification, because predator alarm calls cross both modalities." Dad sawed with his knife. "Still, the differences between the two repertoires are striking. Territorial birds compete and exclude. Flocking birds cooperate and include."

"This is the really cool part," I said.

"We've long known that this behavioral switch is hormonally mediated. What we haven't known is what exactly the hormone does to the brain. The prevailing theory is that the territorial hormone is excitatory. Birds on territory are in a constant state of sexual arousal. It's only when the hormone dissipates that they can access the cooperative behavior of flocking."

"I'm following you so far," said Dad.

"Dessert," said Mother.

After dinner, Dad started clearing the table. Robin rose up to lend a hand. I had to wave her off. Best not to tamper with well-established rituals.

Dad washed. Mother dried. They both argued.

"For Chrissake, they're in graduate school!"

"Still. Not under our roof."

Since the house wins all ties, Robin was bedded down in Alice's old room, as Mother preferred. As we kissed goodnight with toothpaste breaths, Robin said, "I never got to the important part. About the winter robins."

"I know, sweetheart. Maybe tomorrow."

Chapter 2

Alice sat on a bench in Venice Italy, weeping. It was only Venice technically, since it was a bench in the train station. The end of the causeway from the mainland. From there you take a boat to get to the Venice of doges and gondolas and canals. The echoing hall bustled with throngs arriving and departing. Foreign couples immobilized by the sheer weight of luggage, like barges in the human stream. Around them zipping like pilot fish were hotel advance men, Italian, impeccably dressed, accosting anyone who displayed a momentary hesitation to show them a brochure, in English. Clean, cheap, and right off San Marco Square. If their prospect didn't respond, they immediately switched languages. And brochures.

The human current eddied around Alice, keeping a safe distance. She advanced her lamentation from rolling tears to sobs, burying her face in her hands. Her body loosened and the sobs came with her breath. Silent sobs at first, like coughs, then wracking convulsions of grief, her body bending into each, like some orthodox prayer to despair. Her hands fell away from her face and wrapped around her chest, as if to hold her very soul in. Raising her head, she gazed out across the station hall through the clouding water in her eyes.

Then she noticed she was not alone on the bench. "He is not worth your tears." An Italian man. "A beautiful American lady like you. For him to treat you like this." A handsome young Italian. Alice sobbed. "To treat a woman so beautiful like this. He is blind. He is not worthy of you."

"What?" Alice croaked out through her tears. Her image of him was streaked, unclear. The white shirt with the open buttons. The red coral on the golden chain. The chest shaved bare as a woman's. Alice twisted away from him on the bench. The voice continued.

"He does not know you. He does not understand. To make such a woman make tears this way." The voice was soothing, almost kind. "He thinks this is his right. He thinks you will fall down to this. That you will do nothing. Sit. Sit like a dog. Sit and weep in Venice." A couple palpably in love passed by the bench, an arm around each other's waists, their free arms pulling roller suitcases like prospective children.

"Venice is beautiful. You are beautiful. You must not sit and weep. Not in Venice. Not for such a man."

"Was ever woman in such humor wooed?'" said Alice.

"*Mi dispiace*. I did not understand."

"Was ever woman in such humor won?'"

"Yes. One. You are one. Alone. But Venice. Venice is no place to be alone."

"Richard III," said Alice.

"You must not think of this Richard. He does not think of you."

Alice daubed her eyes with a lacy handkerchief. She said, "Would you like a cappuccino? I could use a cappuccino."

At the Bar Stazione her Italian ordered their cappuccinos from the barman, which he then gallantly carried to a table in the far corner. Coffee, she knew from her weeks of experience in Venice, costs more when drunk at a table than at the bar. She had a sudden impulse to just run away while his back was momentarily turned. She could foresee how this scene would play out. She quelled the urge to flee. She was, after all, an actress. And she really did need a coffee.

"Ah, *il cappuc'*. This is the real Italy."

"Actually, I came here for the art."

"*Ecco.* Art. She is the real Italy. Come, drink real Italian coffee. Then I will show beautiful American woman real Venice art. Very special. I know many people. I show you to art the tourist people never see. Very *esclusivo*."

"Actually." Alice was beginning to enjoy herself, the physicality of weeping fading quickly into the past. "I am not here to see art."

Her Italian stared into his little cup, swirled it once, twice. It was like watching the feet of a swan from underwater. "Ah. *Venezia.* Ponte Rialto, palazzos, gondolas! All of Venice is art! The stones of bridges—art! Come, *bella*, I show you."

"I'm kind of here for The Biennale."

"Biennale? The *arte nuova*?"

"Contemporary art."

"*Si*, temporary art. You do not want to see this. You are beautiful. This art is not beautiful."

"It is not worthy of me?"

Her Italian pushed back his chair. "I think you are not serious with my heart. I see American woman making tears, *in lacrime*. I think I try show her some happiness. Come. I tell you my name. I am Mario. So."

"You are Mario, and I am Alice."

"Alice. That means…"

"Yes, I know. Anchovy. This little fish is here for The Biennale. Not to see art. To be art."

"Now I am *confuso*."

"The American pavilion has an installation by Serrio. A huge turntable. Round, *come questo*." Alice pointed to the café table. "On the turntable a car, *una macchina*, but the car is wrecked."

"*Rotto*?"

"No, more than that. Crushed, crumpled, flattened. *Un gran incidente*."

"*Claro*."

"And also on the turntable. Me. I speak about the car, its speed, its power, its sleek lines and responsive handling. In English. And in Italian. And I weep."

"*Tu piangi*?"

"Make tears."

"This is art?"

"It's a living. The problem is that I need to cry in front of many many people. Weeping has always been a very private thing for me. It's hard to do it in public. So I thought the train station would be a good place to practice," said Alice. "Maybe it wasn't such a great idea."

Mario stared down into his now-empty cup. Alice wondered whether his pride was injured. Would he tell her that his heart was wounded and storm out of the bar? He might even slap her. But he didn't seem the type.

"Alice. *Brava. Sei la bella attrice.* When you make tears, I am decepted. I am convinced."

"Thank you. Takes one to know one."

"Again, *non capisco.* This I do not understand."

"Of course you do," said Alice. "You're a *papagallo.*"

"I do not know this word."

"It's Italian. It means parrot."

"Yes, Italian. But I am not this thing."

"You almost had me at first. I thought you were just an ordinary horny Italian. A hazard to navigation. But then, I realized there's something more here."

"Alice. *Bella.* We are become too serious here," said Mario. He pulled his chair in closer. "You are lucky you meet me, Alice. Not some other. I am not like those ones. The ones who do not like women," said Mario. "Alice, I do like you."

"Thank you. Believe or not, I like you too."

"I try always to give the women happy. Always I give the woman the organism."

"Orgasm."

"*Si.* Sometimes I think Mario is too soft. But I cannot help this thing. It is a need. To see woman happy."

"A *papagallo* with a heart of gold."

"Alice. Enough of *teatro.* Theater. Come, let us go to beautiful Venezia. I show you best beautiful things. All day. Then I give you the orgasm."

"Thanks Mario. It's a lovely offer. But my dance card is filled," said Alice. Then she said, "Oh crap. I'm late!"

CS

"Now remember, when we get off the train, let's not get separated," said Robin. I was finishing the spiral for Verona. Not that I ever expected to use it again, but I had gotten into the habit of filling out my maps with what had happened in each place. A kind of journal. Where we kissed Where the fake romanticism of Romeo and Juliet had ceased to enthrall. Where the true romanticism of a city half-engulfed in wildflowers had taken root. The tortoise remembers where he has been. On the little table in the train compartment were a dozen small spirals that had been my actual navigational aids. What I was working on with my four-color pen was the Big Verona, with its many sub-spirals branching away like fiddleheads. It was, in its own way, a work of art.

Alice would meet us at the train station. We would take a water taxi, a boat that was really a bus, to Venice. A city without cars. Or motor scooters. Or right angles. A city half canal water and half little strips of land, all braided together with innumerable bridges.

The train came to a halt. I folded up Big Verona, grabbed our bags and followed Robin. Followed her into the vast reception hall of the Venice train station.

I had a childhood terror of strange places until I realized, late in adolescence, that almost every place is a strange place. Terrain that most would call familiar retains an essential strangeness for me.

Most locales never quite become known; they just feel somewhat less unknown.

In a truly strange place I'm less conspicuous. In an Italian city I can wander at will and I'm no more lost than the typical American. I don't speak the language, but that's not such a drawback. Asking for directions would be rather moot in any case.

When I realized that getting lost in an unfamiliar place felt better than getting lost in my own neighborhood, it was truly liberating. There was no shame in it, and the tortoise was released to wander at will. And to hope for the best.

Sticking close to Robin certainly seemed like the best plan. Meeting up with Alice at the train station. Also a good plan. Alice knows Venice. She's been here since April, rehearsing.

But Alice wasn't at the train station. I looked for her everywhere. Robin made sure that I looked in all of the available everywheres. No Alice. The railway noise and continuous rush of people going elsewhere jangled the nerves. And we were stuck in the middle of it all until my sister could guide us out of there. But there was no Alice waiting on the benches in the station.

"Are you sure?" said Robin. "Perhaps you saw her and didn't recognize her."

"My sister? Are you implying that I wouldn't recognize my own sister?"

"Well I can't recognize her. I've never met her," said Robin. Which was true enough. But I didn't appreciate the undertone of that remark. Especially when she followed it with "Try looking harder. For once in your life."

The train station surged with clamor and bustle. It was no place to have an argument. But I was provoked. "How" I asked her, "am I supposed to look harder? I've looked at every single person here who could remotely be Alice. And none of them remotely is Alice." I stood up on a wooden bench. "Do you want me to yell out her name at the top of my lungs? Would that satisfy you? Would that make you happy?" From my elevated perch I could see a uniformed officer crossing the crowded room. Northern Italians do not stand on furniture.

Robin was doing her best to pretend that she didn't know me. I doubt anyone was convinced, but the gesture didn't improve my mood. I jumped down from the bench with a resounding American boom, grabbed our suitcases and set off at a determined pace. I had her damn luggage. Robin could follow me for a change. Tourists jumped out of my way as I marched across the concourse. Beggars and con artists took a step in my direction, then thought better of it and pivoted off.

I truly had not the slightest idea where I was going. But I was in Venice, so why would that matter?

For once it felt like we were equals. And we'd stay equal at least until Alice showed up. Robin rated somewhere near zero on the Alice Recognition Spectrum; she'd perhaps seen an old graduation photo of her at my parents' house. Which might help if Alice showed up wearing a mortarboard. In rather stark contrast, I have excellent facial recognition skills. It's a separate part of the brain, the fusiform gyrus, as my brain-dissecting girlfriend would no doubt remember, if she just used her own brain for half a second.

I slowed to a stop in that thronging noisy terminal. If Robin was following her suitcase, this was her chance to catch up. Then it would be my opportunity to point out that spatial blindness and facial blindness were completely different. But I refused to look behind me. Like Orpheus. On principle.

A weaselly little man in a gondolier's hat tried to hand me a brochure. Not very effective when both of my hands were keeping a tight grip on our baggage. He tried again with a fencer's lunging motion. I spun in a circle with suitcases centrifuging out to parry his publicity. And I saw my Eurydice. Across a crowded room. Talking to Alice. Like reunited sorority sisters. Both of them ignoring me.

In the starring role of clever little sister, Alice apologized for her delay, a detour that she had apparently already explained to Robin with that kind of shared laughter that women reserve for each other. In the supporting role of older brother, I received a hug, no explanation, and tickets for something called a *vaporetto*. Together we strolled out of the station to the dock.

This vaporetto was a boat that never actually stopped. It slowed down just enough for the nearest and bravest to heave their possessions aboard, which you then pursue as the boat bobs and chugs away down the quay. Already a salty fish in this watery world, Alice knew the exact sharp interjection and hand gesture to hurl at the vaporetto captain. He, of course, ignored her, but did so with genuine respect. Somehow, we all got aboard.

The sun shone, the water sparkled, an endless parade of ornate palaces appeared and as suddenly disappeared at every turn of the canal. *Unexpected Vistas*. Little watery paths branched off the main canal, their wandering waters lapping the walls of these grand treasure houses. It was all so beautiful, and regardless of how many pictures you've seen, still utterly new and fresh.

I reached over to Robin's hand, half-afraid she was still angry with me after my ridiculous behavior in the train station. The tortoise remembers where he has been. And is contrite. I silently forgave Robin her trespass, as I hoped she would forgive mine. Blessedly, she took my hand. I am a field of wildflowers.

Mostly, she benignly ignored me and continued her conversation with Alice. A conversation which had, at the point where I entered, already shed all its proper nouns, subsisting entirely on pronouns. Which, no doubt, was clear enough if you knew the context. I was a bit lost.

But Robin clearly liked my sister Alice. And Alice clearly approved of Robin. And I kept seeing lions with wings.

I pointed them out to Robin, as a matter of ornithological interest. A new species to add to her life list. We went under a bridge. The sound changed. The shadow sadness flooded in for a moment, dispelled a second later as we emerged into sparklers of maritime sunlight. Lesser boats zipped out of our path with the casualness of water bugs. Flooded alleyways with the front doors of houses opening right onto open water like an elaborate prank. Pigeons wheeling. A humped bridge changed its mind mid-span and veered off in a "Y" of alternate destinations. And I relaxed in a way that I cannot remember experiencing before. None of this terrain made any sense at all. I found that immensely comforting. Another winged lion. Not a sphinx. Certainly not an angel. Or a monster. Or a fantastical bird. Something that truly didn't make sense. A lion with wings.

We disembarked from the vaporetto and Alice made a bee line for our destination. She had arranged for a pensione for us in a palazzo on a piazza. But finding any one of these three depended upon finding the other two.

For me, of course, it wasn't difficult; it was outside the realm of possibility. So I was just along for the ride, carrying baggage over footbridges, following Alice's lead.

Except Alice couldn't be certain of any of the three. Alice, plucky Alice, experienced in the ways of watery Venice, got just as turned-around as any tourist on their first day in town. Perhaps we distracted her with our chirping commentary on the miraculous passing scene. Perhaps. But Alice had found this guesthouse for us the day before. She had talked the price down and talked us up with the proprietress, landing us somewhere in the vicinity of the actual going rate. So all was arranged. All she had to do was to find it again.

It has always been a private pleasure of mine to observe other people being lost. Not that I wanted Alice to be bewildered, for her sake and for ours. But through no fault of mine she couldn't find her way. Which left me free to observe.

Displaced people get impatient with the landscape, as if the place they are seeking is deliberately trying to hide from them. It's as if they expect to call out "Marco!" and have the pensione respond "Polo!" And then get annoyed when it doesn't. While I have no doubts that my sister is brilliant, her response to losing her way was surprisingly conventional.

Marco Polo was a Venetian adventurer, not a swimming pool game. He was intent on finding what was out there, once he got lost from all the people and places that he knew. That left him, and me, free to observe all the small and unfamiliar details. Tag, you're it. Alice, with her rabbit pride on the line, wasn't observing much of anything. Which is a necessary precondition for staying lost.

Alice wasn't observing Robin. But I was. The sun came out of the clouds, and she smiled at me, the train station seemingly forgotten. What I think she was trying to remember was if my geographical affliction was hereditary. Had my tales of pathfinder Alice only been relative to my more acute lack of locating? Was Robin really lost in Venice with matching siblings two, without a map, without a clue?

"Oh there it is," said Alice, as she spotted the pensione like a strayed dog that had found its way home. Alice is as normal as they come in the spatial sense. People like her are never errant, it's the roads that wander, the streams that meander. And there we were, standing in front of our home away from home.

Alice introduced us to the owner of the pensione, a stout Venetian woman of indeterminate cynicism. She scrutinized our passports, matching one to the other, seeking clues. In passable English she recited the house rules, announcing each prohibition like an intriguing new idea which she abruptly refused to consider: "Smoking in rooms? No. Visitors overnight to sleep? Not ever. Entry after midnight? Most strictly not allowable."

Our room was small and nondescript, but comfortable enough. The bathroom was down the hall. With the emphasis on "down." To be precise, the W.C. was an add-on, projected outward from the stairwell landing between the two upper floors, hovering over the canal. I wasn't so much concerned about whether the drains flowed directly into the canal as I was by the real possibility that the entire room might break off from the building and sink. But unless that happened, I was pleased to note that I would have no trouble finding the bathroom.

Most of what happened in Venice after that might not have happened if Alice was also staying in the same pensione. But Alice was housed in the Biennale Village with the other members of the American delegation. She had to work the afternoon shift on the big turntable. She would rejoin us later, but until dinnertime Robin and I would be on our own.

Alone together in Venice! In a room with a view, of sorts. Almost overlooking a canal. It was a Romantic Situation. We both felt it. So naturally neither of us knew how to respond to the moment.

It's another kind of lost when two are converging as one, each with heightened expectation of an interlude ecstatic and beautiful. Some full expression of your re-found love. And forgiveness. There's no opportunity to stop and ask for directions.

Robin moved to the window and looked out, observing the sliver of canal that sparkled in the Venice sun. Two-foot-wide sections of watercraft slid into and out of her restricted view. She cooed like a Venetian pigeon each time she glimpsed a boat glide briefly between the obstructing buildings. I failed to see what was so exciting about being inside and seeing bits of boats outside, when we had just been outside seeing the same boats navigating all around us.

But if it was happiness to Robin, it would be happiness to me. I put my arm around the warmth of her waist, leaned my head toward hers and waited for the next boat to show itself.

"So what did you two do all afternoon?" said Alice, when she came to take us out to supper. I grinned like a fool. Robin actually giggled. "I see," said Alice. "Worked up an appetite?"

My kid sister led us to what she described as an authentic Venetian restaurant. Not a tourist dive. We ate outdoors at a wobbly table set on the cobbles. Part of the restaurant's authenticity was that it looked out on neither canals nor bridges. It anchored one end of a small, largely empty piazza. In the exact center of the piazza was a well. In Rome they would have built a fountain. In Florence they would have erected a statue. In salty Venice where fresh water was precious as gold, an old stone well, capped with an iron cover. A Venetian water view.

The waiter came over and Alice ordered for us. I knew better than to try to decipher the menu. Alice assured Robin that everything she ordered was seafood, not poultry. Overhearing us, the nondescript local scrounging birds grew bolder, hopped in closer, lying in wait for crusts from our bread. We drank Friuli, the local white wine.

Around the time that we started making very American jokes about the chef having gone off to catch the fish, our dinners arrived. The food was wonderful. And kind of horrible. It depended on your perspective. I was the recipient of a rather spiky fish, cooked whole, that challenged all of my engineering skills to disassemble. A fish with one appraising eye staring up at me from the plate to make sure I did the job right. Robin got *polpo in suo tinto*, which Alice translated as "octopus in its own ink," a mass of spaghetti dyed ebony in a glutinous pitch black pool with tentacles rising out of it like adolescent science fiction. Alice had ordered for herself something almost normal, a heaping platter of pasta studded with shellfish. And I had to wonder why the shells had to come with the shellfish. Perhaps the kitchen was understaffed, leaving much of the work of turning sea creatures into seafood up to us. When we could actually wrest a forkful from our plates, the dinner was undeniably delicious. Though Robin struggled with the idea of eating black food.

The whole process of dining got smeared somewhat by the excellent and plentiful white wine. And by conversation that flew as lovely and elusive as the small bats that flitted high above the darkening piazza. By evening's end, we all staggered a bit off compass point as Alice guided us safely to our door.

That night Robin and I made love fiercely and tenderly as the cascading images of Venice melded and swirled like Vivaldi's violin of the seasons. Like a true Venetian explorer, I ran my fingertips over every single inch of her skin. They lingered in fragrant meadows and made cautious descents, then pressed on to map the furthest extents of the territory. Robin sent out search parties to intercept my expedition and gather me in. Our hands entwined and held, then came apart again with mute-pressed final touches of farewell. In her I am never lost. By her I am always found.

ᙣ

The next morning began early, as it always does with Robin. She is, of course, a birder. And they are early birds. Whatever flocked to Venice she was determined to find.

So I began my Venetian spiral. I couldn't rely on my little sister conducting us everywhere in this city. My dignity and her employment would not permit. In the exact center of the spiral is this bed. Everything spirals out from there, then spirals back in. I added the room and its door. And through the door the corridor and stairs and the bathroom pendant halfway down. From the bath landing the doors to other rooms, the stairs down, the breakfast room, the view of the canal. I added that watery alley to my spiral map.

By the time Robin had finished her strong black coffee I had cartography drawn all the way to the outside door. Always look at both sides of a door. I ended the spiral there and put a new sheet of paper on my clipboard. To map the rest of the city.

On a sun-filled morning this city of stone and water sparkled. With a tourist map and an eye for the beautiful detail, Robin stepped forth into Venice. With my clipboard and four-color pen I shadowed her, making my own record of the voyage out.

I knew from long experience that conventional maps were all very well and good (in other people's hands) for leaving home base, conveniently marked with an "X". You knew exactly where you started. But when the light shifts and it is time to return, that pretty tourist map becomes a snare of ambiguities, small errors piled on errors, worse than useless. Things look different when you come the other way.

It's then that I pull my clipboard from my courier bag with a flourish. And my Venetian spiral leads us home. A hero of navigation. At least in my own imagination in the light of morning.

We found our way to Piazza San Marco, where everything was up in the air: pigeons in flight, a tall pointy red brick tower with no apparent purpose, a pair of standing columns disconnected from anything else. Walking into the square, the water view was framed by these two dizzyingly tall pedestals. On one, the statue of a man standing balanced on the back of a crocodile. Whatever he's doing up there, his spear is pointing the wrong direction to do that crock any harm. The other pedestal is topped with yet another lion, a seagull perched on his extended tail—both of them with wings. Just beyond it, the open gray-green lagoon water lapped on weathered marble. Smell of the sea. A man bounced a soccer ball on his knee, once, twice, thrice. A pink marble palace in a pattern of diamonds. Next to it bronze horses tucked away on a lofty cathedral shelf threw leggy hoof shadows. Rounded oriental arches, gilded Biblical mosaics, dome after dome, spire upon spire. All so beautiful. And incongruous. Like all the landmarks in the world were piled in one place. We stood in the midst of it all. With hordes of tourists. Seagulls whirled and pigeons wheeled. I knew I should be looking at the guidebook, but frankly, there was too much to see.

Off on the far end of the square, men in official-looking green jumpsuits with matching high rubber boots were unloading sections of wooden walkways from an anomaly. The only motor vehicle in Venice, a forlorn-looking little flatbed truck, a Piaggio with no place to go. They started to cry out "*acqua alta!*" over and over. Then I started to understand why everything in this square was so high overhead.

Sea water began quietly creeping across the pavement, filling the spaces between the cobbles. I watched it, mesmerized, as the lagoon reclaimed Venice stone by stone. The green jumpsuits continued their task of laying down elevated boardwalks and roping off areas, as if the Adriatic Sea was being queued up to go through passport control.

I turned to Robin with what seemed at the time a witty comment. And she wasn't there.

I turned in a complete circle where I stood, rotating until I passed the crocodile column twice. Robin was nowhere in sight. I looked down as seawater began sending little exploratory fingers around my shoes. The green jumpsuits began shouting at me and gesturing for me to move. But I was there and Robin wasn't there. I remained rooted to the spot, my sneakers slowly taking on water. A piece of flotsam adhered to the left one. I reached down and picked up the floating paper. A tourist map of Venice. A waterlogged tourist map with smeary notes in ballpoint pen. A list of bird species sighted thus far.

Retreating from the water and the shouting workers, I backed away across the piazza, keeping my eyes fixed on the spot where I had last seen Robin. There must have been hundreds of other people fringing the slowly flooding square, but beyond quick glances that told me that they weren't Robin, I noticed nothing about them. They made way for me as I continued walking backwards until I tripped up a marble curb and into a wicker and metal chair at a café table. Knowing that the spot I last saw her might be lost if I shifted my gaze, I stared desperately at that too-empty place in the middle of the watery piazza.

"Would you care to order, sir?" I recall now that his English was impeccable, too good to be authentic. But at that moment it didn't register at all. He repeated, this time with a little more inflection in his voice. If they were words, they didn't mean anything. He persisted, first in apparently flawless German, then in Paris-perfect French.

I expected Robin to rise from the encroaching waters, like some great graceful aquatic bird.

Dutch. Spanish. Then something else, not-quite-Spanish, Catalan or Portuguese? A long pause. I glanced quickly at the tourists now crowded on the raised portico that bordered the piazza. I was grasping for a recognition, calculating how far I swiveled my neck so that my sight could return each time to the same point mid-piazza. Japanese. An even longer pause, tinged with a certain asperity. Then the same meaningless question, this time in Italian.

Where did Robin go? I couldn't imagine her just wandering away. Perhaps she saw the water coming before I did and stepped out of its path. After all, regardless of what else she is thinking or doing, there is a tiny anatomical part of every woman's brain that is thinking about her shoes. But she wouldn't leave without telling me. Stranding me there. Absolutely not. But maybe she did say something. And I simply didn't hear it. That could have happened. That listening piece. It's a little fold of male brain anatomy that flickers on and off like a defective fluorescent fixture.

"Sir, you can only sit here if you order."

I pointed to something on a neighboring table. The waiter responded in what was apparently grammatically-correct Sign Language for the Deaf. He returned after a short interval with what turned out to be the most expensive cup of coffee in Europe. I curled my hands around it for warmth. As it grew cold, I shivered.

Hours passed. She should have returned by now. The tidal water was starting to ebb away, leaving pigeons to thread their way between puddles. Tour groups, led by a furled umbrella held aloft, began to venture heroically across the piazza boardwalks in bunched-tight snaking lines.

Robin knew the drill. We'd practiced it many times: if we got separated, I was to stand still and she was to come find me. So she should be in the middle of Piazza San Marco, being annoyed that I had moved.

My discreet waiter returned for perhaps the twentieth time. Confident that he had gotten it right the first time he asked in distinctly American English, "Can I get you anything *else*, sir?"

"Yes," I said, "a policeman."

"Of course, sir."

For what seemed like several more hours I continued to stare at the endlessly varying foreigners peopling Piazza San Marco. Undeterred by the Adriatic, they ventured to cross the puddled piazza on the elevated duckboards. Tourists in single file. Not one of them was Robin. After staring at thousands of people, I had a sudden awful feeling that I had forgotten what she looked like, that she might have crossed my field of vision a dozen times, unrecognized. At some point my cold cup of coffee was removed by a deft and unseen hand.

Then a man in a blue uniform was sitting in the other chair at my table.

"Lieutenant Detective Carlucci," he introduced himself. "The Carabinieri. Are they involved?"

"Oh God." I said, the word conjuring kidnappers, mafiosi. "I don't know."

"Interesting," he said, taking out a small looseleaf notebook.

"We're just tourists here. Americans. I've no idea who that is. The Carbinetti? Do they do things like this?"

"Given the opportunity, certainly. Carabinieri. They're the police."

"I thought you were the police." His uniform was comfortably rumpled in a way that looked authentic.

"I am. We are." He lightly tapped the brim of his hat with two fingers. The waiter brought the middle-aged officer a tiny cup of steaming black espresso.

"We were out there, in the middle of the square…"

"I can't take testimony until I've resolved this matter of The Carabinieri." He sipped through his peppered moustache. "If you didn't speak to them, could somebody else have?"

I shook my head.

"We have to be assured about the Carabinieri," he said. "Jurisdiction." With a second sip he finished his coffee. "If they've somehow managed to open a file, the Polizia Statale won't be able to lift a finger." Ruefully, he eyed the empty bottom of his little cup, then returned it to its dollhouse plate. "It is your good fortune that Maurizio," he gestured significantly to the waiter with his cup and saucer, "is a man of a certain—what would you say—*prudenza*." He placed a fingertip below one eye, significantly.

"So. Testimony." He said, setting his cap down on the table, then unscrewing the top of an exquisite fountain pen. "Yet. Before you begin, I have need to tell you. Venezia is a very safe place. We do not have crimes here. Be reassured. Nothing very bad has happened. Yes, on occasion money evaporates, and who can say? A pity yes, but this is not crimes. Not like Chicago."

ༀ

And so I told my story. From time to time, Lieutenant Detective Carlucci wrote single words in his little notebook, then screwed the cap back on his fountain pen. He seemed in no hurry to wrap up my testimony and get on to solving the case. I spasmodically spun out dire scenarios. He raised a calming hand as if to say this type of thing cannot happen. Mostly he took little sips from tiny cups of espresso. I answered his questions, sorting Robin out from women of other types that he enumerated: Women with sudden uncontrollable urges to shop. Women who abruptly veer off to take a perfect photograph. Ladies who take forever in a lavatory. I reminded him that she had been gone seven hours. He raised his shoulders in the universal gesture of It's Not Impossible.

"I am a long-married man, so what do I know? But were I you, I would go back to your hotel. There you will find one of two things: Either your Robin is there, or her luggage is gone."

Officer Carlucci reached into the pocket of his blue uniform. He produced a small digital camera and took a photograph of my snapshot of Robin. And then he took my photo. Rising, he picked up his hat from the table and held it aloft to Maurizio the waiter, who gestured back like an old friend or an accomplice. Then he handed me his card. It had a small map printed on the back.

When the bill arrived moments later, mine was indeed the most expensive single cup of coffee in Europe. Fortunately, I wasn't charged for the multiple espressos of the Polizia Statale.

I drew the clipboard from my courier bag. Without Robin, I felt the bone-weary familiar sensation of lost. And a second sensation layered over it, a deep indifference to getting found. I was doubtful she would be waiting at the pensione. Robin is not a sit-and-wait person.

I aligned myself with the lofty crocodile. I found the first next proximate point. I began to retrace my map in the other direction. Spiraling back in.

Following from reference to reference gave my mind something to do. And my feet followed. Doing something purposefully helps one believe there is a purpose to doing it. When I again looked around, I was, miraculously, standing in front of our little hotel. I found the key in my pocket. That phrase like a ditty played over in my head: I found the key in my pocket. I found the pensione in the palazzo on the piazza. And found the key in my pocket. The tortoise poked his head from his shell and put one scaly ragged foot forward.

I raced up the stairs, past the semi-detached bathroom. That Robin was here felt certain. *Hope is the thing with feathers that perches on the soul.* Arriving on the landing I came to my senses and double-checked on my map. This door. This. I found the key in my pocket.

No one was home.

Robin's suitcase was splayed open, its upper surfaces ruffled. But had she been back here, or was this the morning's disarray of things? I ransacked my memory. I had absolutely no way of knowing.

I needed Robin to tell me if this or that item was something that Robin was wearing, that Robin would have taken. Just the essentials. But what were The Essentials? I realized I didn't have a clue.

Toothbrush! If she had taken her toothbrush, that would mean something. I unwound my route back to the precarious W.C. No toothbrush. But doesn't Robin often carry her toothbrush with her during the day? Or is that a memory I just invented?

I went downstairs. I had hopes of seeing the pensione manager. She might have seen something. Taken note that Robin had stopped by this afternoon, borrowed a key, broken one of her many house rules. There was no one to be found.

Spiraling back out, I arrived again at Piazza San Marco. I stood in the same spot, as if I could conjure Robin by sympathetic magic. The crocodile aloft was just as trodden and defeated as he was this morning. Here and there were pigeon feathers on the pavement, tumbling slowly across the plaza propelled by the sea breeze. It smelled of brine and receding tide.

Maurizio was not working at the café, but someone who could easily have been his twin brother was. I held out the Polizia Statale business card to him. He studied it for a minute, then nodded as if this sort of thing happens every day and vanished. Before I had soaked up the last of the warmth from my cup of coffee, Lieutenant Detective Carlucci was standing by my table.

"There is progress in this case. Come, you will be more comfortable at the office of police."

I followed this rumpled guardian of the law, my mind dizzy with hope and foreboding. He led me to his office.

Having never been to a police station, I imagined it to be full of battered metal furniture, swivel chairs, file cabinets, in and out baskets, and pedestal fans. It wasn't. Carlucci's office was furnished with two formal chairs, a heavy wooden desk richly enscrolled with carved garland and winged infants, and nothing else. On this vast empty Renaissance tabletop, as if it belonged there, was the latest model laptop computer. On the screen my photo was displayed.

He pressed a button and the photo was projected onto the wall. "*Ricordi*? I made this picture of you this morning. Observe." He pressed another key and the contours of my face were outlined in sepia. Another keystroke and the outline started filling in with finer lines, crosshatching defining with shadow the shapes of nose and cheek and chin. And another thing was happening. My face started looking better. The deer-in-the-headlights stare in the photo transformed to a calm, even contemplative gaze. The program relaxed the forehead furrows and balanced the crooked mouth. The photo itself disappeared and there projected on the wall was my portrait. This was no Registry of Motor Vehicles. Much as I blush to disclose it, I looked handsome.

"Technology," said Officer Carlucci. "You Americans, with your Gates and Jobs, your Brin and Musk, you think it is all in your pocket. You imagine we Italians are the younger sons with the handed-down shoes. You forget. Volta, Torricelli, Marconi, Fermi, Ferrari." Carlucci moved his finger on the laptop touchpad. The discreet ceiling-mounted projector responded. My portrait on the wall nodded up and down in agreement. "I let you have a secret. You are able to understand the genius of Italian technology when you understand that technology is about desire." He slid his finger and my image rotated from full face to three-quarters, to profile. "When the great Marconi came to America, he requested to meet your professors, your engineers, *certo*. But before he sailed to your shores, he also wrote to request meetings with beautiful women." He continued to rotate my head, the back side blank as an egg, to display my other profile. "Olivetti. Ferragamo. This is not 'sexy technology' as you call it; Italian technology is sexual." He smoothed his salt-and-pepper moustache with thumb and forefinger. "An American would never design a Lamborghini."

He rotated my image back to full face. With a final touch of the mouse, he shifted the vantage point so that we were looking down on me from high above.

"We were able to mathematically match your image to our surveillance video," Officer Carlucci replaced my portrait with a white rectangle of light. "Our cameras are quite discreet. Completely silent, of course. We add the movie film sprocket sound when we project them. Because we can."

He pressed a button and the film started to run. It was a view from above looking down on many people milling around, like a documentary of an ant farm. I was confused. It didn't look like Piazza San Marco. It was the Venice train station, St. Lucia. And there I was. And there was Robin. I was gesticulating. She appeared to be trying to calm me. I jumped up on a bench and stood above her, gesturing in wide menacing arcs. The camera zoomed in. She took a step back from me, then another. I jumped down, crouched like an orangutan, then grabbed our luggage and stomped out of the frame. The camera zoomed in closer on Robin. She stood in the middle of the train station St Lucia, quite alone.

"So," said Officer Carlucci. "This is not a matter for the Polizia Statale. Women. They remember things like this. And then..." He shrugged eloquently. He pressed a computer key and the wall went dark.

It only took me three attempts to get out of the police station. The first time, I stumbled into a dayroom where officers were playing cards. My second attempt brought me to the end of a corridor where a clerk was asking a distressed tourist whether the purloined Euros had any distinguishing marks. On the third try I found myself outside.

The pink lanterns of Venice were now lit. The morning's duckboards had been discreetly removed. In the half-light the Piazza still thronged with tourists, but their pace had slowed to an Adagio movement. At the Caffè Florian, the music played on. I walked out into that vast open space.

ೞ

I pulled out my clipboard and started a new spiral, putting that point in the exact center of the page in four-color ink. On the outermost reach of the paper I wrote the name "Robin."

To the extent that I could tell, absolutely nothing in Venice was on a grid. This gave a distinct advantage to my way of mapping. In steady tortoise fashion, I went from the place I was to the next place that I was, always careful not to come back to a place I had already been. Because I never crossed my own path, I proceeded in my version of a straight line. Which seemed to be Venice's notion of a straight line.

When I came to water, I crossed it. Then I turned around and noted how the crossing looked from the other direction. All of this went into the spiral notation in blue ink. Always look at both sides of a door. I crisscrossed paths with families of visitors going back the way they'd come, looking for their lodgings, arguing over a piece of folded paper. I said to myself, "I am not lost in Venice. I know exactly where I'm not."

I spent my second night in Venice alone, with Robin's suitcase for company. I felt lost.

Chapter 3

In the morning I went looking for Alice. In due course I came to a vaporetto stop. I marked this in red to indicate my good fortune. Like all buses, the vaporetto goes from point to point along a tortoise path. It can't take shortcuts. You can abandon any concern about where you are; you just have to know at what stop to get off.

At least that's the theory. But transit bureaus mar this elegant simplicity with express routes and directionals and transfer points. Routes run only on certain days, certain hours. Schooled by experience, I bought the all-day pass, not the single ticket.

I scanned the list of stops for Biennale. I wanted the #1 boat. Simple. Then I looked for the floating bus stop. They were lettered "A" though "D." Did the #1 boat go to the "A" dock? There seemed to be no way of knowing. A vaporetto was approaching. A crowd of people were trying to get ahead of each other in eagerness to board. So far as I could see, the imminent boat didn't have a number on it anywhere. It stopped at the nearest wharf to where I was. So I got on.

Somewhere far from Venice, out in the open water of the lagoon, there is a weathered bronze statue. It is two men standing in a stylized boat: Dante and Virgil. Crossing the waters of the damned.

Ᵽ

Biennale. It means every other year. On even-numbered years a hundred or so countries fill their permanent pavilions in Venice with nationally representative art. So Spaniards can sneak a look at developments in French art, and vice versa. That's how it all got started, according to Alice.

And then something changed. The art got political. Art that made a statement on the policies and the culture of its representative country. Then it got meta-political, expressing the futility of expecting high art to influence the culture or policies of its host nation. Then it got meta-meta-political, commenting sarcastically on artists believing they weren't implicated in the things they objected to, owing to the fact of their entitled position as art makers. This led to ironic meta-meta-political, art that dethroned art-making by embracing naïve art, blatantly commercial art, and the simply tasteless: Banality at the Biennale.

One more step would have probably brought it full circle: meta-ironic meta-meta-political art, which would celebrate the finest in nationally representative art as a commentary on all of the above. But this was a bridge too far for the artistic community. They collectively recoiled in horror from the idea.

None of this was in evidence when I got off my fourth vaporetto at the Biennale stop. What struck me first and forcefully were the trees. Neatly planted rows of mature trees, hundreds of sycamores whispering greenly in the sea breeze. Amongst the trees neat gravel walkways in rectilinear patterns. Cloth banners snapped in the wind, red with white lettering, announcing Biennale. Beyond the trees and banners and ticket booths were the pavilions themselves, each the fruit of a modernist architect playing with blocks. The most un-Venetian part of Venice imaginable.

I went to the ticket booth. There was no one there, just a dispensing machine and an intercom button. I selected a language and pressed the button. I said I needed to see my sister. The pre-recorded message said it was in the Venezuelan pavilion. I said, not "My Sister," my sister. Works in the United States pavilion. A recording read me the list of works in the United States pavilion, then went silent. I pressed the button again. I explained that my sister was employed by a United States artist as part of "American Entropy." There was an "America: Entropy," is that what I meant? I said yes. The recording said showings are on the hour. I said, I didn't want to see the art in the American pavilion, I had to see my sister, now. There was silence for a moment. They suggested Venezuela.

I finally convinced the informational machine that I wanted to see a person, not a painting. The voice said I would have to go to the staff entrance. It was on the other side of the Biennale. The intercom went silent. The machine dispensed a map.

I walked a short distance away from the ticket entrance. I jumped the fence.

It was hardly a high security perimeter; it was a chest-high row of cement planters full of impatiens. I came down with a thump on the other side, turned back to the planter and began to annotate my spiral map with this relevant landmark. A security guard was walking in my direction. My first impulse was to run. He had seen me climb over the planter. But running had never gotten me anywhere except hopelessly lost. So I continued to make my map. Apparently, nobody jumps a fence and then turns around and sketches it. The guard treated me like I was a Biennale artist. As if I didn't exist.

Every fiber of me said hurry. I needed to find Alice, to spill out everything that had happened. Once again, my kid sister would know what to do. Somehow Alice would find Robin, just as she had at the train station. I cringed at the memory of my behavior at the train station. Had Robin really left me over that? It looked so much worse on video than I remembered it.

I had to suppress the rabbit. To find Alice I would have to go slowly, working my methodical way across the exposition grounds until I found the United States pavilion by process of elimination.

Heaven helps the fool—when God has run out of other options. I came across the American pavilion almost immediately. I entered between the Doric columns of the surprisingly conventional Greek Temple of Art facade. Turning into the first gallery, I found Alice inside, sitting on the edge of a huge turntable in a blue sequined sheath dress, drinking a tiny cup of strong coffee.

I began spilling out my tale. Robin's sudden disappearance, my vigil in the café, the first meeting with the police, the empty pensione, my second encounter with the police. I made a first, largely incoherent, pass through the material, and I was just going back to tell it over again in something approaching chronological order. Alice held up her hand.

"I have to go on," she said. "After this performance, I'll get Monica to take over, and I'll be yours for the afternoon. Lewis. Don't go anywhere."

So I sat and watched my sister coo seductively about American cars while tears rolled down her cheeks. In that amphitheater audience I sat as alone as I had ever felt. And I wept.

When Alice had finished and had made arrangements with Monica, she reappeared in normal clothing and ushered me into a hushed gallery dominated by a monumental statue of the mascot of the Big Boy franchise, holding a burger aloft on a platter.

I told her the story again. Alice immediately knew what to do. "Have you checked the hospital?"

"Oh God. I hadn't even thought of hospitals. Surely Lieutenant Detective Carlucci would have checked. And anyway, we were in the middle of Piazza San Marco. How could Robin have ended up in a hospital?"

"Simple," said Alice. "The *acqua alta* came in. She slipped on the suddenly wet pavement. Went down, banged her head. Got put in an ambulance, taken to the hospital."

"Alice, there's no way I wouldn't have noticed an ambulance in Piazza San Marco."

"In Venice, ambulances are boats."

"Still," I said.

My sister was uncharacteristically silent.

So we contacted the hospital. They had no record of Robin being there, either admitted or treated and released. No record of anyone even vaguely matching Robin's description being brought there yesterday. At Alice's Italian prompting, they checked the ambulance records. There was no log entry of a pickup anywhere near Piazza San Marco at the time of the *acqua alta*.

"Lewis, let's go to the pensione. See if she's returned back there. I'll bet you a *bombolone*—a cream-filled doughnut—that she has."

I didn't much feel like a doughnut, though the mention of it reminded my stomach that I hadn't eaten in over twenty-four hours.

Alice led us out of the Biennale site, past the Paradise Café and down to the vaporetto dock. I blanched a little at the thought of putting myself back at the mercy of this utterly baffling transit system. Alice had no such hesitation.

We got off the boat at the stop nearest our hotel. I began leafing through the sheets on my clipboard. Alice said, "I think I can find it, Lewis."

She did. We went upstairs and surveyed the room. The bed was a disaster, something I had to take responsibility for. I had tossed and turned all night. Robin's suitcase was seemingly the same as before. But she could have come and gone several times, picking up and dropping off changes of clothes. How would I know? Could we simply have been missing each other? I regretted not having left a note for Robin on her suitcase.

I expressed this to Alice. My sister took one look around the room and said, "She hasn't been back here."

Alice sounded very sure. Sure as Sherlock. So I played Watson. "And how have you come to this conclusion?"

"Elementary, my dear Lewis. It has grown colder in the last twenty-four hours. If Robin had been back here, she would have picked up warmer clothing."

I looked at the rumpled surface of the suitcase. "Since her lame-brained boyfriend has no idea how many sweaters or jackets she brought, how then do we know whether she has come back here and removed one?"

Alice looked at me like she suddenly realized that I was a guy. It wasn't a flattering look. It was a look that said that the two of us have entirely different standards of obvious.

"Look at the room Lewis. A guy might pop in and pick up a jacket. A woman doesn't do that. She *selects* which jacket she wants to wear. To select a jacket she has to put it on. To see how it looks, how it feels. So if she had been back here, there would be at least one jacket lying somewhere outside her suitcase, the jacket she decided not to wear."

One way to avoid conceding a point to your kid sister is to suddenly be busy doing some necessary task. I started picking up my dirty clothes from the floorboards.

"And another thing," said Alice. "If Robin had been back here, she probably would have made the bed."

I composed a note to place prominently on Robin's open suitcase. At least I tried to write a note. And I remembered another note, left in a teaching assistant's office, back when our journey together began. With any communication, you have to know, or at least assume, what state of mind the recipient is in. I didn't know what I could assume. So, again, I just wrote the facts: "Found Alice. Lost without you. I love you."

Left to myself, I would likely have stayed in the room, waiting. A tortoise sitting at the fork in the road waiting for someone else to take one path or the other. This, of course, is not Alice's way. Before my note was finished she was out the door and vanished from sight down the corridor. In pursuit of something. Like a detective in a paperback.

I called after her and Alice answered. So I asked her a question, some bone-headed thing about how you say something in Italian. Then I called out another miscellaneous word, like she was a walking Pimsleur phrase book. And in this way I followed the sound of her voice. Out of the rented room, her words passing doors and down hallways, echoing in stairwells and then released into the clear air of Venice.

"Where are we going Alice?"

Alice stopped in her tracks. Like I had asked her why she was wearing shoes. Apparently the answer to my question was so obvious to her that it didn't bear mentioning. "To St. Lucia."

"The patron saint of the blind?"

"The train station," said Alice. I was startled by the arrival of a vaporetto just as I realized that we were standing on the floating boarding dock. Alice handed me a ticket that she had somehow materialized, and we got on board.

"Everyone," said Alice, as we took our seats and caught a whiff of marine diesel, "except for the very wealthy and the very local, come in and out of Venice at the same place. The Stazione St. Lucia and the parking lots and rental cars surrounding it."

"Yes." I said, feeling a wind from what felt like a very long time ago. "Robin and I came through there. Of course you know that. You met us there." It was my chance to be the older brother. "Sis. The train station is absolutely mobbed with people. All the time. Even if we somehow knew when Robin would pass through there, we'd have something approaching zero probability of spotting her." Alice was obviously showing her Hare side, thinking that just being in motion was somehow getting us closer to the goal.

"We're not going to the train station to look for Robin. We're going to the train station to look for someone to look for Robin."

"I see," I said, not seeing at all.

"The police don't know where she is. Because there was no crime," said Alice.

I thought miserably about the train station, Detective Carlucci's closed-case scene of the crime.

"The hospital doesn't know where she is," Alice continued, "because there was no accident. With no crime and no accident, who would notice Robin amongst so many people?"

I shrugged. It seemed like the answer she needed. Alice continued.

"Someone who would notice her. As a very beautiful woman. Who is obviously a foreigner. And unescorted." Alice jerked us to our feet as the vaporetto arrive at the St. Lucia dock named for the saint of Girls Who Wear Glasses. "Hold onto your hat, Lewis. I'm taking you to the dark side."

Inside the train station, Alice directed us to the little coffee bar in the corner. In the far corner of the bar, she approached a rather too louche young Italian man holding hands with a rather too vivid older woman from some north-eastern corner of Europe. The Italian visibly blanched when he saw Alice bearing down on him.

"*Fratello!*" she cried out.

Whatever the Italian man was expecting, that wasn't it. His face went as blank as if he had just been handed a photocopied algebra exam. Alice raised her hands in the international gesture of 'of course you know me'.

"*Sorella?*" said the Italian. "*Si!, Sorella mia!*"

Alice made a bee-line for the vivid lady, her hand extended. My sister the actress. She spoke in English with a fraudulent but convincing Italian accent. "Such a pleasure to meet a friend of my brother. It is sure I don't need to tell you. We are fortunate who know him. Would you not agree? A gem. So thoughtful, so *simpatico*. Please. I wouldn't think of intruding," said Alice, doing exactly that. She motioned me toward a chair, maintaining her standing grip on the bracelet-jingling paw of the now somewhat less vivid woman. "We are so lucky that we meet you here. Mario is so often busy. He with his work. Eh? And all Venezia. You would concur? No?"

"But he said. Giovanni," the woman puzzled in Berlitz-school English.

"Of course. Giovanni. Gio. We call him Mario. For short. In the family." Alice added her free hand to the grasp, giving the woman's hand an assuring double pat before its final release.

"Gio. Mario," Alice said, completely swiveling her attention. "It is Mother. Again. We tried. But she insists that only you." A tear trickled down Alice's cheek. "You are so good to her."

"*Sorella?*" said Mario. Not algebra. Calculus.

"So. We walk your dear friend to her hotel." said Alice picking up the stranger's magenta soft-sided suitcase. "We will write down the number. For later." she continued, turning to go. "Because Mario. Well, you know."

The four of us stepped into the bright Venetian sunlight. I was more than happy to get away from the Santa Lucia train station. All

I could think about were video cameras mounted high up on the walls. And Robin.

Who this Venetian was, and what he had to do with finding Robin was beyond me. He didn't seem like a Biennale guy. But maybe I just have preconceptions of what artists are supposed to look like. And Mario didn't match them.

As we walked over a bridge to the nearby hotel, Alice explained our situation to Mario. She clearly wanted this oily Italian to do something for her. And the Italian wanted to slip out of it. But somehow Alice seemed to hold all the cards. With a backwards glance, Mario reluctantly left the vivid woman at the reception desk.

I didn't even try to keep track of where we went after that. Alice told Mario that Robin had vanished in San Marco. Mario led us somewhere else entirely. Two vaporettos were involved. We ended up in a part of Venice that tourists never see. Because there is nothing to see there. At least in the Venetian sense of nothing to see. We stood before a plain stucco two-story building with a faded plexiglass plaque that said "Venezia AC".

"Air Conditioning?" I said.

"Associazione Calcio," said Alice. "Soccer."

OK, I thought, a soccer club.

"The Lagunari. The lagoon dwellers," said Alice.

Mario chimed in "*si*".

"This is not exactly a soccer town," explained Alice. "Think about it. Where in Venice could you play soccer? A sideline kick would inevitably skitter the ball into a canal. Venetians are watermen, rowers. And since they are at least nominally Italians, they are also rabid soccer fans. But with little help from the Lagunari. The worst soccer team in Italy."

Mario sighed. Whatever part of this he understood was plenty.

Mario pushed open the door and we followed him inside. When our eyes adjusted to the dim light, we could make out tattered black banners with green and orange stripes. Black and white photographs in dust-hazed frames. All of it appearing to suffer from decades of neglect. On one side a heavy oaken bar with an elaborate old-style brass and nickel espresso machine.

"*Ecco*," said Mario. "*I Lagunari.*"

From somewhere behind the bar there was a rustling of newsprint, like the sound of an interrupted rodent. "Americans!" a creaky voice spat out. "We read about your Cubs of Chicago, your Red Boston Sox. And you Americans call these teams cursed." A dismissive crinkling of paper. "Cursed because they do not win games? Only a smug nation of winners would call that a curse."

We looked over the bar toward the source of this derision, and discovered an ancient barman seated on a folding chair next to a second chair piled nearly his height with newsprint, sports magazines protruding from the midden with a glossy glimpse of colorful jersey.

"I Lagunari. This is a squad under a true curse. An Italian accursedness. A bane worthy of Guiseppi Verdi.

"There on the wall you see the pictures: 1941, champions of the Coppa Italia. The first and last time. In the spring of 1941 all Venezia is exultant, just as Mussolini's army was falling apart in North Africa. We are Venetians, we live in the reeds, with no belief in Roman

Fascist glory. Even so. It began then, the avalanche of humiliation for all of Italy.

"Eight years pass. Defeat, occupation, poverty. The squad of '41 was broken up, the Orange-Black-Greens dispersed to other cities, other teams. Yes, but still we play the Beautiful Game. Then, 1949, eve of the national championship, the entire Turin soccer team."

The voice broke off abruptly.

Mario looked at the walls, avoiding our eyes. I looked at Alice. She shrugged.

"So," I said, "what happened?"

The barman addressed us like school children. "The Titanic was a big boat. The Hindenberg? A zeppelin. A tragedy? Torino, the beating heart of the *Azzuri*, Italy's national team, were returning from a match. The Turin plane missed the runway in the fog. It didn't miss the House of God. The Titanic hit merely an iceberg. Torino was killed to the last man by slamming into a basilica. Above all, the brilliant Valentino Mazzola, team captain, the greatest Italian football player of all time." A sigh of infinite loss, evergreen. "His midfield partner, Ezio Loik. United in death. The two last former members of the Lagunari of '41.

"Now you believe in curses? In 1971 Venice's stadium was destroyed by *il tornado*." Alice confirmed that I heard that right; it's the same word in Italian. A tornado in Venice.

"The stadium? She was never actually rebuilt. It is discussed endlessly to this day. They make a few temporary seating.

"Then the president of the Venice club bought the Palermo club. Next week he exports all her best players to Palermo. To Sicily. Pah!

"Then the first bankruptcy. One, two, three foreign owners. Demotion after demotion to smaller leagues.

"Next, the match-fixing scandal. The lagoon-dwellers were already relegated. Yet still they were bribed to toss away a game that they would have lost anyway. Not just paid to lose. That would not be enough humiliation. Paid to lose to Venezia's bitterest foe. Not some petty rivalry of sport, but the hated adversary of centuries, our foe in wealth and trade and power, our only rival in mastery of the seas: Genoa! (May her name be lost to History.)

"Naturally, a second bankruptcy followed. Then in her wisdom the Serene Republic condemned the ruins of the stadium as unsafe. It is on an island. It was sinking slowly into the lagoon. The team, of course, was well-known to be unsound. The soprano plunges the dagger home. Final chorus in minor key. Curtain."

Mario looked shyly over at us, all of his machismo melted away, his eyes wet as a spaniel's. "*Grazie*, Fiorino. While you live, all Venice may yet hope."

There was a sound of rheumy throat clearing from behind the bar.

Alice prompted sodden Mario, who wiped his eyes with a handkerchief. He addressed the barista. "Piazza San Marco…" And he explained in Italian why we were there.

The report of the barista spitting. "Where is the one only place in Venezia big enough, flat enough, unobstructed, to play the Beautiful Game? Piazza San Marco. And where is the one place in all Venezia for playing *calcio* is impossible? And prohibited strictly? Piazza San Marco.

"Nevertheless," said Fiorino. "We are Lagunari. Eternal. We pray to San Marco for protection. And we play in Piazza San Marco. The squad dresses before dawn. This is youth, this is glory. As the cafes set out their tables and chairs on the cobbles, the Lagunari scrimmage. This is against the law. But so are lions with wings. The Orange-Black-Greens finish as the tourists start to arrive.

"The tourists stare at the Palace of the Doges, at the bronze horses on the cathedral. The Lagunari sit in the cafes at their ease. They sip endless cups of espresso. They are Venice. The café owners refuse all payment. These are young men. They give no attention to the pink stone of the Doges. They *fare la civetta*."

"Make like an owl?" said Alice.

"*Si*. All eyes, all turning neck. They look, look, look at all beautiful women. If anyone," said Fiorino, "saw your Robin, it was the Lagunari."

Chapter 4

Robin

Lewis was saying something about flying lions when I spotted a great white egret (*Ardea alba*) from the vaporetto. Global citizen, not to be confused with our snowy egret. Two species of gulls: the *Larus* genus, of course, and black-headed *Ichthyaetus*. Aside from that, Venice is an empty habitat. Opportunistically filled with pigeons. Not native here, or really anywhere; thriving everywhere as immigrants.

It is true, there's an undeniable fascination in a world where water defines the terrain. Here the land mazes through the waterways, rather than the other way around. Take away the buildings and bridges and you'd have a salt marsh.

But the people who colonized this salt marsh took a wrong turn somewhere and kept right on going. Piazza San Marco. A grand open plaza surrounded by beautiful architecture. Burly mechanical men with hammers ring out the hour atop the great clock face. The boom of the bronze bell rings across stone pavement, reverberates off the colonnades that mark its perimeter.

Yet. Not a single tree. Not a bush. In all this vast public space. Not a hint of grasses dancing with the current of the inrushing tide. No surprise: not many songbirds here.

Lewis seems enthralled with it all. It's beautiful architecture. So very beautiful. Maybe just not my kind of beautiful. But take this opportunity. Let Lewis guide you, come to see what he sees. Isn't that what love is, seeing what he sees, enlarging what you love with what he loves?

I want to give him something to remember this day. Maybe months from now, on his birthday, or on no special day at all, I want to have a gift for him that will bring him back here.

But naturally there's a problem. When you travel together you're joined at the hip. Never an opportunity to slip off and purchase that surprise memento. Lewis being the way he is, it's even less likely. But even he can't get lost standing in one place in a huge open space. There's a vendor right over there. A kiosk on wheels, the frontier of retail right out here in the square. I hand Lewis the map, tell him I'll be right back.

It's amazing how many things she has in this little portable kiosk. And that's not the only amazing thing about it. Apparently Japanese tourists return from Venice Italy sporting T-shirts in English touting Florentine art. Everything is in English, with the occasional substitution of "Venezia" for Venice. A T-shirt emblazoned with "Bigger than David"? Not promising.

Then I see it. A map of Venice silkscreened on a T-shirt. But not just any map. A stunningly intricate maze of tiny winding streets and vivid blue branching canals. And floating above it all in the most official typeface imaginable, the phrase "You Are Here." Lewis would love it. At least I think so. Anyway, I'd love to give it to Lewis. I just have to find his size.

I'm waiting to get the attention of the proprietor as she negotiates the sale of a stack of junior gondolier wear with a very persistent German grandmother. The seller writes down a price on a little pad. The German writes down a different price. The vendor feigns shock and disbelief. Writes down another price. And so forth.

Across the piazza someone yells *Acu Alt*, or something like that, and the other vendors take up the cry. My kiosk tender rapidly concludes her international negotiations. My hand is outstretched toward my intended purchase. She goes to the far side of the retail cart and begins determinedly tugging it across the piazza.

The thing about shopping while traveling is if you see something you want you must buy it at once. You'll say to yourself that I'll come back here and buy it later. Resist it. You won't. You'll be struck by the thought that you'll find the same thing elsewhere for less money. Resist it. You won't. Unless, of course, you do buy it. Then, naturally, you'll see it everywhere.

So I follow after the vendor. Her portable shop is incredibly noisy, rumbling slowly across the cobbles. And I fall in behind. Stalking a boxy wooden construction six feet tall and four or five feet wide. She can't see me. I can't see her. But the T-shirt is right there before me. As soon as she stops, I'll be her first customer.

And then the rolling box accelerates. It's moving at a brisk walk and surprisingly I can barely keep up. Whoever is pulling it, it's no longer the woman who was selling the T-shirts. We trundle into a side street, then right, into an alley. Moving now at a furious pace.

Then, abruptly, the box reverses direction. Moving backwards, directly toward me. I duck into the open shopfront of a little store selling Murano glass to avoid being run over. Incredibly, the box keeps coming at me, turning, trundling right into the shop. The little glassware store is barely bigger than the kiosk. I'm forced backwards to the rear of the shop. All around me there are glass shelves display-ing hundreds and hundreds of fragile objects. Directly in front of me there's a huge wheeled wooden box. Somehow they've maneuvered it into this narrow space without more than jiggling this kitsch of colored glass lining all three walls. I hear a click and the lights go out. I yell out "Hey!" The metal roller door comes down with a rumble and a slam. And I'm in the dark. All around me little glass gondolas tinkle.

☃

I should have started shouting at once. Perhaps then whoever locked me into this shop would have come and let me out. If it had been a leather shop, I probably would have. But there was something about the sound of that first yelp of surprise. It reverberated in that confined glass-lined space. Mirrored walls, glass shelves. It bounced around in there. As if I wasn't shouting out to whoever locked me in, but more like I was yelling at myself. And what I was hollering was *why are you such an idiot?*

My second reaction was anger. I hadn't done this. This had been done to me. I was mad enough to throw a gondola. I grabbed some-thing up, massy and glassy in the pitch dark, and was about to heave it at the plywood kiosk. But then I remembered my martial arts training and re-centered all that energy. Those imprisoned in glass houses shouldn't throw stones. With each breath I became more a warrior, less a victim. *The first opponent to overcome is always yourself.*

I began feeling along the edges of things. Perhaps there was a back door. Or a back room. Which maybe has a telephone. Or a light switch. Inch by inch I navigated the glass-lined walls with carefully tentative hands. When I arrived at the edge of the rolling kiosk, I measured with my spread fingers the gap between the shelving and the box. Not wide enough to slide myself through. I started walking my hands back around the other direction.

My sleepwalker's legs bumped up against the shop table. I felt nothing on the tabletop. There was a drawer. It was locked. But I had given up the idea of breaking things. I explored beneath the desk and found an entire library of folded boxes lined up on end, arranged by size and shape. And something that felt like packing excelsior. A cord ran down the back leg of the table to a socket in the floor. I unplugged it. Nothing happened. I plugged it back in. Nothing happened.

I made no further discoveries. There was only one way out and it was blocked. Quite literally by a big wooden block. I inched my way back to the table, slid down to the floor. From under the desk I pulled out an armload of packing straw to cushion the hard ceramic tile. I made myself a little nest.

That's where they found me in the morning.

With an enormous clatter the roll-up metal front wall rolled up. Bright daylight made its way around the kiosk box. "Hello?" I called out. The metal shutter rolled back down. Once again I was in utter darkness.

An eternity later the retracting security shutter was again thrown open. The overhead lights blazed, blinding me. When my eyes adjusted, I saw the rolling kiosk, the store within the store, and someone peering around it at me. Reflected in countless mirrors was a man in uniform with a very large, very black, very deadly looking submachine gun.

I put my hands in the air, like they do in the movies. Someone tugged the rolling T-shirt bazaar out of the shopfront. The cop stepped into its vacated space. His uniform was pure couture. White leather Sam Brown belt crisscrossing his black tunic, red-trimmed epaulets, scarlet piping down the seams of his sharply creased trousers. On his head was an ebony policeman's cap with a silver badge: a bomb with a blazing fuse.

He certainly dressed the part, but he didn't seem to have any notion of what to do next. Far from being square-jawed and decisive, the young patrolman was pimple-faced and looked like he would rather be somewhere else, picking olives.

He gestured with his still-impressive Beretta submachine gun. The gesture was less an order to march as it was an admission that it wasn't possible to shoot me inside a glass shop. Maybe if I moved somewhere less fragile he would be able to reassess his options.

The kiosk proprietress and a stocky muscular type, apparently her husband or brother, started telling the policeman what to do. In rapid-fire Italian. In great detail. Finally, the boy in uniform swung his Beretta behind him on its sling, then tentatively approached me holding a pair of handcuffs at arm's length before him. He cuffed my wrists with my hands still in the air. Which meant that when I lowered them the only comfortable position was to hold my hands in an attitude of prayer.

He picked up my floral purse from where it had served as pillow for my nest on the floor. He slung the bag over his shoulder, where the skinny strap immediately entangled with the sling of his big ugly black weapon. His pimply complexion reddened, embarrassed to be carrying so girlish an accessory.

In any other city, I would have shortly thereafter had my head ducked into the backseat of a squad car. But this being Venice, the arresting officer had two choices: parade me on foot to the station house or hustle me on board a police boat.

Walking me at gunpoint down the winding alleys and over the innumerable bridges of Venice was clearly not a real option. You could see his acne blossoming at the very idea: in the thronging tourist streets the possibility of my escaping (or him losing me) was enough to give him pause. Discretion argued against it as well; capturing me was not worth the innumerable visitor photos taken of my perp walk across Venezia, with him sporting my flowery purse. And somewhere in the back of his gendarme consciousness was lurking the embarrassment of getting lost himself enroute to the station house.

But in Venice police boats are few and far between. Clearly my captor did not have the clout to have one at his beckoning.

So we traveled to the precinct house by gondola. He sat facing forward, I facing back toward the hired gondolier, placidly plying his oar. Both acted as if this was a perfectly ordinary way to transport felons. When we passed under the Rialto Bridge, people waved gaily.

With my manacles, the best I could respond was a flutter of fingers like the wings of a captive bird.

The gondola docked at a water side door on a side canal framed by gray granite and smoked glass, with the word "CARABINIERI" inscribed above the door. After some negotiations with the gondolier, my arresting officer gunbarrel-gestured me from the rocking boat into an austere lobby, from which three corridors radiated. At the hub of it all was a desk emblazoned with the same symbol as my officer's cap, a bomb with a flaming fuse. I was handed over to the desk sergeant for questioning.

But it wasn't me that was questioned. It was the arresting officer. He stood awkwardly before the desk and received a dressing-down such as could only occur in the Italian language. In this torrent of words his shoulders gradually drooped lower and lower, like a songbird on a branch in a rainstorm. In the brief intervals when a response was possible, my pimply captor responded in sullen monosyllables.

Certainly all this had been a mistake. My arrest at gunpoint. My imprisonment in a glass-shelved souvenir gallery. My pursuit of a rolling shopping opportunity. Even the T-shirt was probably a mistake. In retrospect, would Lewis find the humor in wearing a map he had no hope of comprehending?

The sergeant behind the desk waved my policeman aside with a sweep of his hand. Dismissed, he skulked off down the left corridor. With my purse. Tenting his nose with his fingers, the desk sergeant gestured me forward.

"Venezia is a city of judicial codes, not of arbitrary ukase. Did I use that word correctly?"

"I'm not sure. It's a very obscure word."

"*Bene.* Back to where I began. Venezia. You have been arrested. What we are yet to know is for why you have been arrested."

This seemed the moment to plead my case. "It's all a mistake. Their mistake. I didn't do anything." I tried to gesture my outraged innocence. The handcuffs told a different story. "The simple fact is they locked me in. If anything, I'm the victim here."

The officer continued his thought as if I hadn't spoken. "The Carabinieri have a reputation to uphold. Because this is so, we come again to the question. It is not should you have been arrested, but for why you have been arrested. This requires reflection."

There's only so far you can push me before the Irish in me starts pushing back. "Let me get this straight. You're saying I'm under arrest because some idiot with a gun arrested me? And that now you can't un-arrest me. Why? Because that would look bad? Did it ever occur to you that what would look even worse would be this? Arresting the victim of some stupid Venetian shopkeeper?"

The officer in charge didn't so much as blink. "In your country is it common for owners of businesses to find persons unknown to them curled up in a nest inside their shops when they open the waterproof security shutters? This is not normal behavior. And what is not normal is a violation of the accepted course of civilized society. An infraction."

"I was locked in all night!"

"Yes. This is very helpful to the Carabinieri. With your assistance we now have The Infraction. Violation of Civil Code 33-A14 (amended), sleeping in a public place not authorized for overnight accommodation."

"I wasn't planning to sleep there."

"Italy is a country of laws. Those laws are based on actions, not intentions. If laws were based on what we did or didn't intend to do, then where would we be? So. We've just established which one you violated. This is progress. Italy is a country of laws. But Venezia, Venezia is a city of tourism. And you are a tourist. So it can be seen we have a dilemma. You stayed overnight in a place unlicensed for hospitality. And yet you are not one of those unsightly backpackers, one of those *Europe on a Budget* vagabonds.

My arresting officer returned with a sheet of paper, and my passport, wallet, and purse. He placed them on the desk. The desk sergeant glanced at the paper, then continued. "You booked accommodations. You have assets. According to this, your credit is exemplary."

"You ran my credit cards?"

"Purely as a precaution. We wouldn't want to hold you falsely as an indigent. As a point of factuality, this being Venezia, and the law being fulfilled, we don't want to hold you at all."

"You ran my credit cards?"

"*Signorina*, we are the Carabinieri. That title alone gives us broad discretion in such matters."

"So am I expected to sign that paper to authorize a ransom against my bankcard, or do you have 'broad discretion' to do that too?"

The desk officer flipped through the pages of my passport, avoiding my glare. Then he set it down, resting his hand atop it. "Miss, this is not the scene in the bad movie where the corrupt Polizia takes the bribe. We are restoring your passport to you, and your credit cards, quite untampered with. One small matter for the fulfillment of the law. Then you will be free to go."

"What 'small matter'?"

"We have to release you into someone's custody."

Custody. Like some errant child. I wondered momentarily whether there were separate penalties on the books for women. Penalties that involved having some man come to claim them. That would be so Italian. Then I thought of Lewis. I felt a rush of relief pour over me. Lewis. I would be released into his custody, we would be reunited. Then I thought of Lewis.

"They have to come here?"

"That's what releasing into custody means."

Assuming I could call Lewis. Both of us had left our cell phones behind in the States, useless on the European network. I would have to call the pensione. Assuming I could reach him there, Lewis would try to rush to my rescue and immediately get hopelessly lost. As we say in neuro-anatomy, men are hard-wired to protect their women. The male cardinal keeps watch on the branch while his lady cardinal flits to the feeder. But how do we wire ourselves to protect our men from themselves?

Then I thought of Alice. Would Lewis find it unforgivable if I called his sister, not him, in my hour of distress? Probably. But it was the only solution that made any sense. I would call Alice and have her go get Lewis, and then the two of them could come and rescue me from the Carabinieri.

Two uniformed men passed through the foyer, toting huge black guns and laughing at some private joke. I asked the desk sergeant to call the Biennale. He did. He handed me the phone.

"Per Italiano spingi l'uno. Pour Français pousse deux. Por Espanole oprima el numero tres. For English press four." I pressed 4 before I could be told what to do in Swedish or Dutch.

"For tickets press 1. For hours and directions press 2. For special events press 3. For interpretive tours press 4. For large groups press 5. For handicap access press 6. For interpretation for the blind press 7. For interpretation for the deaf press 8. For interpretation for the press press 9....For tickets press 1. For hours and..." I pressed zero. Nothing happened.

A patrolman brought in a man who was clearly intoxicated, loudly argumentative, and linguistically Japanese. The desk sergeant shrugged and pointed to the corridor on the right.

I asked him to dial directly to the American Pavilion at the Biennale. He talked conspiratorially into the phone for what seemed like an excessive amount of time. He hung up and turned to me. "That number is not permitted to the public."

"But you're the police. Surely they can give that number to you."

"Of course. They did. For the Carabinieri such matters are a triviality. But we cannot give to you that number. That would be impermissible."

Your first adversary is your own anger. I heard my sensei's voice in my head and resumed my composure.

"If you have the number, then surely you can call it. Yes? And if you can call it, you can give them my message." The sergeant nodded, as if this had not occurred to him, but when examined the notion presented no insurmountable obstacles. I gave him Alice's information, the briefest summary of my situation, and a message for Lewis, telling him that I loved him. The sergeant wrote it all down, as if English was second nature to him. He pressed a buzzer and a clerk whisked the paper away down the middle corridor.

"Now we wait," he said, gathering up my wallet and passport, putting them back in my floral shoulder bag, then tucking it somewhere behind his desk. There were no chairs in the foyer. And no sign of a bathroom. At this point I could use one.

The orderly returned with the text of my phone message. "The person Alice could not be reached. We have learned that people dislike their employer hearing that they received a call from the Carabinieri. The message we left was discreet."

"Cryptic," I said.

"Cappuccino?" said the desk sergeant. He pressed his buzzer and I was led away down a corridor to where coffee awaited. And a room about the size of the back end of a glass shop, in which I was to wait.

Chapter 5

We left the soccer club, Alice, Mario, and me. Mario wove us through little pedestrian streets, his arm tucked in Alice's like two old friends out for a *passeggiata*. I, of course, followed close behind, having no clue where I was or where we were heading. We boarded a *vaporetto* for San Marco. Once there, Mario announced grandly, he would make introductions to Sebastiano, a famous Lagunari.

I began to suspect that Mario's true intention was to give us the slip once we reached a sufficiently crowded location. Alice kept his arm clamped into her elbow, but her real hold on him was a mystery to me.

The mob exiting the bobbing *vaporetto* carried us with them onto the unpronounceable Riva degli Schiavoni. Mario led us past a clutter of souvenir kiosks, then up and over, squeezing through a bridge full of tourists all standing in the center of the span snapping photos of another bridge: the Bridge of Sighs. Which isn't really a bridge at all. It's a short, elevated walkway high above an alley of a canal. It's supposed to be romantic because that's where prisoners went to jail.

Once again in the Piazza San Marco. A sequence of proximate landmarks. I unfolded my spiral map, aligned myself with the pillar of the man balanced on the crocodile. Oriented at last, I fixed my eye on the spot where I had last seen Robin, in the desperate hope that she might somehow be there, waiting. Instead, there was a tourist couple standing in a flurry of birds, pigeons landing on their up-raised palms like a St. Francis impersonation. The birds were less interested in the sightseers' sermons than with the birdseed in their cupped palms. The couple smiled gamely, if somewhat nervously, while a freelance photographer took the souvenir portrait.

I thought of Tippi Hedren and the Hitchcock movie that was my first date with Robin. Though Tippi knew that the birds were only landing on her to peck up the seed strategically placed by Wardrobe, the experience truly terrified her for years afterwards.

Then I felt Alice's hands on my shoulders. She rotated me. On a seat in Caffè Florian facing the piazza was a guy dressed in the or-ange-black-green of the Lagunari. His companion chair occupied by a soccer ball.

Mario made some mysterious Italian gesture, and the soccer player rose and came forward. They locked in a fraternal embrace. They whispered a few conspiratorial words. Then the player turned to me. "*Foto?*" was all he said.

I fished out my wallet photo of Robin and held it in his direction, reluctant to let it out of my grasp. You could see this Sebastiano's eyes flickering through mental images, looking for a match. His con-centration seemed absolute. Nervously breaking the silence, I told him that Robin disappeared yesterday morning, unsure whether he understood a word of English. Guessing that he didn't, I rotated back around to point to the spot where I had last seen her, taking care to align my right shoulder with the crocodile. There was no one there. The pigeon couple had departed. It was a vast open square. And somehow Mario had vanished into it.

Alice rotated me back to Sebastiano. His eyes had stopped flickering. "Yes," he said "This one I recognize. You sit the Piazza, you see people by thousands. Old, young, single, coupled, grouped. Most do not make impression. Every day or two you see a woman of rare beauty, a perfection. You fall half in love. That *bellissima* you remember for always." Then he added, "This one was not one of those."

I was about to rise to Robin's defense. Alice placed a restraining hand on my shoulder.

"In the Piazza couples argue," said Sebastiano. "Usually it is exhaustion only, sometimes something more deep. What you call *rancore*. This makes the attractive person ugly. Fewer times you see people deep in love. This makes the ordinary beautiful. This too you remember. Then you see Love itself. For this it is worth sitting in this café all morning."

He pointed to the photo. "This one I remember because she was touched by Love. Then I see her legs, running after."

"Which way did she go?" I said, then felt the crushing absurdity of that question coming from me.

"That way," he gestured vaguely. "It is not the where that was amusing. It was that she was being led away."

"By a man?" I blurted. Alice gave me a look. So I added "A woman?"

"A souvenir stand. Typical tourist crap: *robaccia*. I try not to notice such things. But they were calling the *acqua alta*. So the seller was moving it. A woman, *si*. This woman was rolling it with the

wheels across the cobbles, her selling finished. And this one runs after. As soon as *bella* got close behind, the *robaccia* would speed up,
just out of grasping. It was what you call cat and mouse game."

"And then?" I said.

"I knew beautiful foreign women would not risk their shoes getting wetted. This ended the game. So I left the Piazza."

"But the girl?" said Alice.

He looked at Alice, as if memorizing her. "Those pretty American legs. Running after a box of tourist crap on wheels."

For a moment Robin was not lost; I could see her in my mind's
eye. Chasing a rolling rumbling souvenir kiosk. It felt like hope.
Then it didn't. Unlike me, Robin would not have gotten lost in San
Marco. Whatever compelled her to chase that vendor across the
square, she would have come back.

I was about to ask some kind of question. But Sebastiano
shrugged, as if to say that life makes no sense. He picked up his soccer ball from the chair. Then he was gone. Vanished like the hopes
of the Lagunari.

I looked about the square. There were no souvenir kiosks to be
found. The light was turning and the branches of pink streetlights
had just been kindled around the Piazza, then the chandeliers up
under the colonnade. The orchestra at the Caffè Florian launched
into "New York, New York", their musicianship far superior to their
repertoire.

Where did the kiosks go at night? They weren't tucked into some
corner of the Basilica. They were, apparently, towed out of the Piazza
by stocky shopwomen in sensible shoes. Then what?

It's my hippocampus. It's a little part of the brain shaped like a seahorse. I had said to Robin on the first day we really talked. I soon learned that she knew far more about the hippocampus than I would ever know. *It's where we map the world around us in space, the ento-rhinal cortex, the Moser coordinate system inside matching the one outside point-for-point. Or not, in my case.*

Then Robin had said something so odd that I wondered whether she was even listening to me. She said, *Do you listen to music with stereo headphones? You should try it.*

I thought back across the last two days to the moment when I realized that Robin was gone. And I could see the moment with terrible clarity: the crocodile on the high pillar; the thronging empty Piazza around me; the briny water oozing up through the cobbles, tracing rivulets from the lagoon across the square; the soggy tourist map wrapping itself about my shoe with her birding list penned in the margin.

"Lewis?" said Alice.

I closed my eyes. I listened to Venice. At first all I could hear was the chatter of a thousand tourists. The scrape of café chairs on cobbles. Then I could hear the slow working engine of the lagoon as its waves struck and restruck the embankment. I pivoted in place and my ears knew where the water was. I opened my eyes. I was facing the sea.

Marco Polo is not just a Venetian explorer. He is also a swimming pool game.

I'm sure Alice had decided that her brother had finally gone over the edge. But I didn't care. I put my finger to my lips. I closed my eyes again. I tried to reconnect to the moment when Robin disappeared. I tried to recall not what I saw but what I heard. Again, the white noise of tourists. The cries of *acqua alta*, high water, in Venetian accents that made it sound more like *"acu alt"*. The slow heartbeat of the lagoon, but a softer more slippery sound as the waves quietly crested the breakwater. Then clear as a bell in my right ear, Robin's voice: "I'll be right back. Don't go anywhere." I startled, opened my eyes. She wasn't there. I felt my eyes well with tears.

I forced them closed again, though it felt I was like extinguishing Robin's presence, phantom though it was. I heard the rumbling of the wheels of a heavy wooden box across the cobbles. I turned in the direction of the remembered sound. It grew fainter and fainter. Then it was suddenly louder, echoing in some kind of tunnel. Then fainter again, less reverberative. Then fainter still, as if heard around a corner, then abruptly silent, stopped. I opened my eyes, I was looking across the Piazza to a small archway on the right side of yet another landmark. The big clock, the *Torre dell'Orologio*. The wild bronze men high above swung and struck the hour with their sledgehammers.

"Alice," I said, "follow me." It was something I hadn't said since she was 7 and I was 9. And which had gotten us hopelessly lost. Miraculously, she did.

I couldn't allow my eyes to stray for a split second from that archway. Anyone trying to take a selfie in front of San Marco was simply going to get run down. I had to trust that Alice was still tagging along behind. I couldn't turn to look. If I did, I knew I would have lost it.

I reached the archway and whooped, hearing it reverberate as I passed through. Straight ahead, straight ahead, don't look at anything, just trust your ears.

Now sound dampens. Make a turn. Left? Right? Is that right or left? Doesn't matter, it's the only turn, so it must be the right turn. 1-2-3-4-5-6-7-8-9 and stop. Here.

I was standing in front of a restaurant, the café tables spilling out to occupy most of the street. I was actually standing between two of the tables. The British couple enjoying dinner at the one closest to me focused on their plates and feigned obliviousness.

"It should be here!" I said loudly. They became intently involved in their *branzino*, as if a fatal fishbone was surely lurking there. Alice came up behind me. "It should be here," I said to her.

Alice pulled me out of the middle of the restaurant. "Look around you," she said. Maybe she just let it slip, but she had to know just how much I detested that phrase. The implication being that if I only started paying attention, if I wasn't so dreamy, then all my navigational issues would somehow magically disappear.

"No, really. Look around, tell me what you see," said my kid sister.

"A fish restaurant. Tables. Chairs. A chalk menu board which I can't read. Do you want me to go on?"

"Yes. Tell me what's beyond the restaurant."

"A leather shop full of candy-colored purses. A display of women's belts laid out like a cowhide rainbow."

"And what else?"

"Nothing. A closed-up shop named Serenissima; I have no idea what they sell. Lagoon-proof rolldown solid metal shutters. Another closed storefront, apparently glassware for the umpteenth time, this one called "Murano"—it really annoys me when people use quotation marks for emphasis."

"And what do those closed-up shops remind you of?"

We both said it at once. "Garages."

Alice took my hand and led me out of the maze of café tables and across the lane to the leather shop. She started idly handling handbags. Sometimes I don't understand my little sister at all. Clearly this was not the time for retail therapy.

The proprietor immediately started to engage her in a description of the quality of his goods. His was the only real leather sold in Venice. Perhaps in all of Italy. All of the others used some debased process, some form of tannery fraud that involved cardboard and magic markers, for all the attention I paid to his spiel. Alice picked up a wallet printed all over with gilt winged lions. She asked him why his shop was still open when so many others were closed. He flattered her taste. She immediately put the wallet down and picked up something completely different. He explained that leather was his only business. Alice nodded like this made perfect sense.

"So the other stores are closed because they run more than one shop?"

"*Si*. When they are closed one business is inside the other business." He made a gesture of dismissal, as if only very second-rate enterprises would put a business in a business. He then proceeded to tell an amusing story about a thief who somehow hid inside a rolling souvenir stand to sneak inside the glass shop across the *calle*.

"But the joke was of her. Having broken into Murano, she had not had thoughts how to break out again.

"Now this is a lovely clutch. Comes with a removeable shoulder strap, see here inside? Two zipper pockets. Here, look, the zippers are double-stitched. Very important. And a secret compartment. Is that your husband?"

"Brother."

"*Bene*. A secret compartment. All women have secrets."

"So what happened to this lady thief," said Alice.

"Attempted thief. There is no crime in Venice. The Carabinieri came. They took her away."

Alice put down the clutch with the removable shoulder strap. She spread her fingers in the universal sign for 'I'm all finished here.' She turned to me and said, "Come on. We have a gondola to catch."

"Gondola?" said the shopkeeper. "Moonlit night. *Signorina*, you are quite certain this is your brother?"

℠

After that, there is not much more story to tell.

There was the matter of the Carabinieri needing to establish relationship before I could assume custody.

"Beloved."

"This is not one of our categories."

"Girlfriend? Lover?"

"There are no checkboxes for these. Perhaps 'Mistress'?"

We finally settled on Fiancée, which wasn't strictly accurate, though it would become so within a month.

Robin and I were re-united. We held each other like we would never let go again. We spilled over with our worries, our fears, our immense relief in tears and in that kind of laughter that is the same release as tears.

And we yelled at each other like a parent yells at a child lost and then found at the supermarket. Why didn't she get my attention before running off? How could I not have heard what she said? And watched where she went? Why hadn't she stopped while she was still in the line of sight? What had possessed her to chase after a gift that I didn't need, probably wouldn't wear?

To make a memory of Venice. Our souvenir of Venice was this moment. And all the crazy painful moments that led up to it. It was not exactly a souvenir to cherish. Few souvenirs are. But it is one that we will gladly keep for the rest of our lives.

As my mother said at our wedding reception the following year—the reception where the caterers forgot half the cutlery and our guests had to eat dinner with tiny cake forks—"If nothing went wrong, what would you have to remember?"

But I'm getting things out of sequence, as I often do. It's a little organ, shaped like a seahorse. I have to take you back to that day in Venice for one last postcard. Like most photos we take on vacation, it makes me look better than I actually was.

Robin, Alice, and I were walking in a square past the ornate red brick facade of an enormous church. It was dedicated to a saint that none of us had ever heard of: San Zanipolo. Our best guess was he must have been Marco's uncle.

And I said, "Let's get something to eat. I hear there's an open air bistro by a pretty side canal just down this alleyway. Follow me."